FAN, INC.

Warning:
Your Oxygen Is Low

A Novella

By
Barbara McVeigh

Contents

Notes

Writing can be a cathartic process to deal with trauma. It is a simple tool to use the trauma in order manifest a narrative for the greater good. The work includes the act and intention of sifting though fears, temperaments, love, hate and quizzical patterns, as well as humor to laugh at absurdities that we as humans can only deliver. It is a way to love and celebrate ourselves even during our darkest times.

Today the art and joy of reading stories has been usurped by the domination of quips and memes, which have virtually eliminated the broader context of meaning and negated the deeper feelings that we have the capacity to explore within ourselves.

We have essentially destroyed the proverbial literary and imaginary forests of shrubs, animals, insects, flowers and streams in order to worship a singular redwood tree, not recognizing that the tree needs the forest for its very survival.

As a community impact artist, I invite you to help rewrite the novel that dominated a society, to cultivate and empower our collective story before the virus of apathy and a sterilized world kills us all from the inside out and we shall never again witness the forest for the trees.

We are nature. We are art. We are human. We write our future each and every day.

- Barbara McVeigh

Chapter One

She fell hard against the large boulder, panting. Her body limp, exhausted. She was more weary than frightened as she began to accept her fate. A fate she was choosing. The monitor attached to her ring finger indicated she had less than one hour of OZ, her oxygen supply.

"Damn, it." she said. But, she felt glad that at least she had sliced the chip from her wrist without instant death. For now, it'd be harder for The MOO to track her. She tightened the bloodied wrap around her wrist.

She glanced around, looking like a wild animal, dirt on her face mixed with blood and sweat. Lost, she tried to gauge where she could be. Nothing was familiar. And, yet it should be. Then, she looked upward and gasped as if confronting the temples of Gods long forgotten. Like Roman obelisks with messages of life and death, testaments of seasons and time, greed and

I

survival. The ancient coastal redwoods towered around her majestically. How brilliant they looked. Strong. And, there they stood as noble as she remembered them. She needed to be with them one last time. To be sure they were real. That something was real.

While looking up, with neck fully extended, mouth wide, she dipped into a childhood memory playing with her little brother, collecting redwood cones and pelting them at each other. How he'd always hit her and make her cry. And, yet, she missed him. Her family. And, what she had thought life would be. Thirty years ago.

Now, just one more hour to live. For the first time in her life she recognized that this one decision was hers and no one else's. Not FAN's. Not MOO's. A decision to die. And, how to die. And, that gave her just a little bit of pleasure. Power she never had.

The long black boots hurt her feet. Blisters were forming as fast as bubbles in a test tube. She yanked them off. Apprehensively she placed her bare feet down onto the cool humus of the ground. The earth felt alive against her soles, like touching the remnants of her own soul, a touch like a lover's body, skin on skin. A simple action that was forbidden. How cruel the laws had become, and nobody else saw them that way. She felt like a renegade, doing the forbidden. Entering The Wild Lands and connecting to nature. Defying her own father.

"I protected it for you, Patricia. I kept it pure, for you," he had said. And, she shuddered remembering her father's words. Patricia had come to understand the consequences of her father's actions now, keeping people silent. Playing God. How she just wanted to go back to her old life. The parties, the shopping. When life was fun and you didn't have to think about anything more than yourself. Thirty years ago. Blood dripped from her wrist, and she tightened the bandaging.

She stood there for moments under the redwoods, just feeling, trying to feel her soul again. But words kept coming through.

"You see, men like John Muir didn't understand society," Father had said. "People can learn independence, self reliance from nature, how to think and care for themselves. But they never do learn how to wipe their asses, so to speak. You can't allow people power. Like children, you must watch them always. No, not children. Viruses. Breeding viruses. Keep them busy, entertained; give them some sense of purpose, if you have to. Remind them who is in charge. Technology did save this planet. And, I have saved it all. For you. And, now you must take on the leadership. The world is yours," he had said the first night he called for her to The MOO Tower.

She breathed deeply again tasting the bay scented OZ that flowed through the mask to her nostrils. It smelled artificial now. All of it, even life itself, contrived, when one is faced with the real thing. All her beliefs, her God. All of it. Gone. Father. Clearly, he commits a crime against humanity, doesn't he? Worse than Stalin? Hitler? Lying to people. Watching people. And, now he wanted her to be him? Nonetheless, here were the last ancient trees, saved. And people had oxygen. It's true; Father had saved so many people from dying. And air, the gold of the new millennium.

"He protected this one patch of land especially for me," she said out loud. "A virgin forest."

She couldn't bare it all. She felt alone in the world too. Just like these redwoods amidst a polluted world that was desperate to generate new life. A grove he had named after her. Why?

"Patricia, don't get me wrong. I protect people from themselves." Father had said.

"FUCK YOU, FATHER!" She screamed. Birds fluttered from the trees. She looked at her OZ. It was almost empty.

She came back to her surrounds and listened for a sound beyond her breath and beeping of the monitor. Were The MOO still following her? She knew they would find her. And, yes, Father would be with them, leading them. Nobody survived the truth. And, who'd ever believe the truth? She understood it all now, except for one missing piece. But that piece was probably a lie, as well. Her sex partner had told told her stories about a colony of mushrooms that'd take over FAN, Inc. and MOO. How could mushrooms destroy anything? She told her Father, and he in turn told her things about her sex partner and showed her images of him with children, blood and sex. There was nobody to trust. God, she had loved him. Skin on skin.

"Stop thinking," she said out loud. "Just feel nature. Just feel. That's all you've got now." The monitor read 45 minutes. She turned off the timer.

Her soft hands rubbed the dusty lichen patches on the boulder. Caked dirt filled her nails, four broken, jagged. Brown, red and yellow leaves surrounded her, resembling a patchwork quilt, like her grandmother had once given her. If only she could climb into it. Fall asleep. Fall. A season. Something she hadn't seen for so long. Not the real thing, at least. How people could profit off the natural seemed so incongruent. She thought of the ubiquitous images strewn around the cities reminding people of the Wild Lands that they were protecting because they no longer trammeled upon them. Life experiences were merely manifested through goggles or porn or MOO's piped in bird songs. How could people worship MOO? They had become the gods who could create and destroy reality. Why must she only think of these unpleasant memories, about what others are too ignorant to even want or think about, when she herself still has opportunity to take in the pleasure of pure nature, one final time?

She paused. "I am my Father's child. One cannot escape it."

She sat down cross legged against roots of a Bay tree, reminiscent of limbs reaching out from the earth. Maybe this is where she should die, she thought. Embraced by the roots of a tree. She touched them, so familiar, so beautiful and so forbidden.

Patricia closed her eyes remembering, listening, and feeling. There was silence at first and her internal thoughts were loud. She kept pushing them out of her mind.

"Listen."

And, as she did, new sounds began to surface. Slowly, at first. A leaf rustled. A beetle crawled over it. Wind above blew through the trees reminding her of the sound of ocean waves, when people were allowed at the seashore. Before all of nature was cut off and trespassing became forbidden in order to protect the last resources. "For the survival of humanity", The MOO, Modern Order and Organization, announced when she was ten, not long after her parents divorced.

"FAN, Inc., Fresh Air Naturally." She let out a laugh thinking of the mockery of it. There was a time when air was free, part of life. Such a spoiled society, she thought. Not knowing what you have until you don't have it.

"Stop thinking, Patricia." She said out loud.

She opened her eyes and looked around. How peaceful The Wild Lands all looked. Like a paradise. They had paradise. But words again kept spinning in her head.

"Patricia, this is not working. Stop thinking. It doesn't matter anymore. Everything is a lie, except for . . . maybe these trees," she said again out loud, as if to The Wild Lands, her only witness. She looked at the wrist monitor again. Twenty minutes now. It was time to decide where to die.

She walked on the moist soil that squished between her toes. Small sharp pebbles stabbed her feet, but she appreciated the pain, a reminder that she is of flesh. A memory of a childhood time. That she is still alive. For the moment.

She came to a stream of water so clean and transparent and dipped her foot in the water, withdrawing it quickly. Frigid water. And, then she stepped in with both bare feet, allowing the water to flow around her ankles, washing her mind away from the immediate past. She threw a pebble and watched the ripples. First there was a small one, but more grew bigger and bigger.

"One simple drop can cause such consequences," Patricia murmurs, remembering her mother's words.

It's all coming to her now. Mother, Father and little brother. The memories of this very place. How she hated her brother. He was always out of control and hitting her. But, Father, he had treated her like a princess. She'd ride high on his shoulders as he told tales about the wonders of the wild. The animals, the plants, and the tiny trap door spiders that lurked behind the moss, monitoring and catching their prey. It was an obsession he had, pointing out the spiders and their intricate webs, the mastery of design. "It's pure art and science," he'd say as he'd watch mesmerized studying the weaving. Patricia tried to save a butterfly once from a web and he yelled at her. "Don't fight nature," he had said and she watched the butterfly fight for its life and he watched in delight. She shuddered as a child. She began to shudder again.

"People don't like them, but without spiders, there'd be no balance in the world, Patricia," he'd say.

He'd talk of the invisible yeast and bacteria suspended in the air. Everything was alive and people couldn't appreciate or respect the abundance. They just wanted more and more. So much was wasted. He hated that.

Mother knew about mushrooms. And, together they'd find sweet candy caps and bake them into cookies. During night walks, they'd spot illuminated jack'o lantern mushrooms. They really did glow. And, once oyster mushrooms lined a log like buttons on a keyboard, or chanterelles popped like trumpets from the ground. Another time they found a grove of prized porcini with caps as big as pumpkin pies. There was such pleasure taking from nature. And, perhaps that's why it was so wrong. They feasted together. Together, like a family. A family. Something that didn't exist anymore. Not for her. Not for anyone. Families were old traditions The MOO had decided were no longer good for society. FAN, Inc. endorsed it.

Patricia walked on, feeling the forest floor tickle her feet. She wanted to smile, to laugh. When was the last time she smiled and laughed? For the first time in years she felt free from watchful cameras, sensors, monitors and tracers. She had only ten more minutes to feel this sense of freedom and then it'd all be over.

The air was still thick with smog but it was better than in the cities. Lichen lay dead on the forest floor. She remembered the old man's beard. Usnia. That native lichen used for tea. The tea her father still drinks.

She remembers finding the lichen hanging on old oak trees and pulling apart the threads that snapped like rubber bands. Oak Trees, just a memory now. They had died of disease like the Chestnut trees long ago. How odd, after so many years, once you know nature, you don't forget. It stays with you. The thought consoled her for a moment, until an alarm brought her back to the present.

The time had come. No more OZ. She sat next to the stream and looked around one last time, as if saying goodbye. Then, carefully she pinched off the tubes from her nostrils and removed her mask, taking her first breath of real oxygen in years. It'd be a matter of time for the cough to set in with phlegm then blood and then death. She stroked the on the rock next to her, remembering her mother's gentle, consoling touch at night.

"Go to sleep now. Away from this world."

She held back any tears. There were none left. There had been so much death. Why couldn't life have been respected? And, then again she couldn't even respect her own.

The coughing began. She kneeled onto soil, looking up at the trees, as if asking for forgiveness from a God. The scent of earthly decay filled her nose and she took it all in, recognizing how good it smelled.

"It'll all be over soon. All gone. No more pain." she said as she coughed.

The sun set behind the redwoods splashing a deep pink hue across the sky. Pink. Still her favorite color after all these years. The pink tones in Autumn leaves, the burst of Naked Ladies in spring and the slick underbellies of salamanders discovered under a reposed, moist log. She remembers.

The nearby babbling brook became a roar, deafening her. She gasped again. Another cough and there was blood. Finally, she curled into a fetus position while her vision grew more blurry and distorted. The pressure on her lungs, as if a spider were binding her with an asphyxiating thread.

"I'm sorry, I'm sorry," she tried to say.

Then there was pressure on her extended hand. A squeeze just as her lungs felt. She tried to look up. A child, a wild child in fragments of clothes sat down in front of her, genitals fully exposed. The child held her hand. Squeezing it. The child looked at Patricia with a cocked head, just staring at her like a curiosity. The child held in the other hand a banana slug like an ice cream cone. She licked it and then extended it to Patricia, like a gift. The hallucinations must have begun. The girl looked up beyond Patricia.

"Not too hard this time, Jimmy," the child said. "You killed the last one."

An excruciating pain overwhelmed Patricia's head. And, all went black.

Chapter Two

First there were low voices. Murmurs. The stench of earth and decay was strong. Dense.

"And, didn't they know what they were doing?" Patricia heard a voice say. She cracked open her eyes to a dark room with flickering light from a small fire and shadows pulsating against the edges of a dirt wall.

"We have very little. If we take what we need only," one voice said. Another voice spoke up, "We can continue to survive but she needs more than us right now. How do we trust her?"

The light was a dingy yellow, mustard like. And thick dust filled the air. Shadows moved with the voices. The shapes obscured. Her head throbbed. She could taste dried blood in her mouth and a tooth wiggled.

She slowly opened her eyes more. The child. There was that child sitting in a corner caressing a head. A small head. And, talking to it. The child hummed a tune that sounded familiar, and then the child looked up to Patricia.

"Do you see her?" the child said, and she approached Patricia, holding the head of a doll out for her to see. The glass eyes stared wide, and the hair was ratted like the lichen of the forest.

"It's gone from her wrist. But, they are smart," that man's voice said from somewhere else. "What about behind her eyes, the implanted camera? If so, we are doomed for sure. Or even in her blood stream, they can inject microscopic tracing materials now."

Patricia looked at the child and they locked eyes. The child cocked her head again, curiously.

"Where am I?" Patricia whispered to the child, trying to be discreet.

"Jimmy! She's awake!" the child burst out yelling. Her voice pierced Patricia's ears and she winced. Her head throbbed. And, then she thought of that name, "Jimmy".

"Where is she? Where is she?" An old woman's voice came from another room. It echoed dully but it was strong, vibrating, sounding desperate. There were thudding footsteps. Clouds of dust building in the room.

"My God! It is her! She has come!"

A person got close to Patricia's face. The breath putrid, making Patricia wince, closing her eyes. Then she opened them again. Face to face with another. A woman. The old woman's teeth were yellow and black.

Her face was like the boulder Patricia had leaned against for strength, one full of deep crevices and dirt.

"Patricia? Is it really you?"

A small group of people crowded around Patricia.

"Who are you? How do you know my name?" Patricia tried to say.

"Jimmy, come here. Right now!" the woman said.

A bearded man appeared before her, equally filthy. His long beard reminded her of the Usnia hanging on the old oaks. A small bug crawled across his forehead, and he wiped it away like a wisp of hair.

"Everybody. Please, join us for this moment! Patricia? Do you not recognize your very mother? The one who gave birth to you?" The woman clasped her hands together, as if she were about to pray. Her fingers were crooked. Fingernails crusty.

"You came like a life force out me, my dear. I remember. You sent me to the emergency room afterwards for two full days. Your father cared for you, and how he loved you. I would have died had you been born one hundred years earlier. Modern medicine saved me. The irony!" She looked up at the crowd, "Of course, that was at a time when women still gave birth," and laughed at what seemed like a joke for some.

The child pushed through the crowd, and reached for Patricia's hand, squeezing it.

"Patricia, I am your mother and this is your brother, James. Do you remember? Tell me you do."

"Am I dead?"

The small crowd laughed.

"Buried six feet under, indeed, but far from dead. How did you find us, my dear?"

"I found her," the little girl tugged on Mother's clothing. "I found her almost dead after her OZ went out. I offered her my slug, but she didn't take it."

"Lily, you have compassion and you are generous, That is good. You are a beautiful child and you have learned well. Was anyone with her?"

"Yeah, Jimmy who clubbed her on the head."

James looked down, as if ashamed.

"Oh, just like the old days." The old woman chuckled. "Times change but people don't, isn't that right, Jimmy?"

"James. Jimmy. My brother?" Still Patricia could hardly believe what she was experiencing. Her head throbbed.

"I'm sorry. But, I had to do it. And, really I didn't know it was you, Patricia. I'm sorry."

"If he is my brother, he never apologized for hitting me. Where am I?" she said with anger and she spit out a tooth. Lily picked it up.

"Finders keepers! Mother!" Lily said, and she ran back to her corner and tried to wedge the tooth into her doll's mouth.

Mother eyed Patricia. Blue eyes penetrating hers. "Oh, you are like your father. I always knew so. But, you are from me too. And, unlike others in this big world of ours, your burden is the greatest. You have responsibility, Patricia. And, you have not used it yet.

You have a legacy and I hope I trained you well as a child. You must now know the lies and deceit, if you are smart like I always knew you to be. You've been living in your Father's world. But, you have come to me now, back to the Earth. So, there is hope for us all."

The crowd murmured and nodded heads. "Just as the prophecy promised" a woman said in the crowd.

Mother looked at Jimmy. "Yes, your brother hits for good reasons now, and he can pack a solid punch," she laughed. "You can take credit that all his practice on you when you were little has helped us all today. Jimmy is a good son and will show you he is a good brother."

Jimmy grinned, looking down to the ground.

"Rest now my dear. We have much to discuss later."

Patricia looked away and up to the ceiling to see worms dangling above her from the dirt ceiling. She gasped.

"What are those?"

"Roots. They are our food. Don't play with them. Did you hear that Lily? Make sure Patricia does not play with the food." Mother smiled. "And, don't you play with them either, Lily." And, mother shook her finger at Lily playfully.

"Yes, Mother." Lily said. The girl was still playing with the tooth.

"Mother?" Patricia asked. "Who is Lily?"

"Oh, I've become the mother of many children. It's a long story. Thirty years. But, we are alive, and like I said, we have hope now. You have come back to me."

Patricia was becoming tired. She had so many questions. And, yet she didn't know where to start. Her head ached and still her lungs felt squeezed and she needed to cough, a danger in her father's world, a sign of disease, a threat to society.

"Lily, one last request. Get the medicine. It will help Patricia," Mother said.

The child put down her doll's head gently and grabbed a banana slug that was sitting on a log next to her. She approached Patricia.

"Lick it," Lily said, thrusting it toward Patricia's lips.

"What?"

"It'll help you. The slug just ate the special mushrooms." Lily said.

"Your stomach will settle more easily," Mother said as she began to leave the room. "We don't act proud here. Do as you need to do."

Patricia stuck out her tongue and the child moved the slug along it. The taste was a bit bitter, and the texture was like a tongue upon tongue. Patricia closed her eyes. Her stomach rumbled with the thought of licking this thing, but then her stomach did get better and the pressure on her lungs eased.

"Sleep now." And, Lily hummed that song again. That familiar tune. And, Lily's little fingers stroked Patricia's hair like Patricia remembered Mother doing so long ago. Patricia slept for what seemed like a long time.

Chapter Three

Something large crawled across her face and Patricia woke with a start, away from a restful dream. Her head itched too. She did not want to leave her dreams, though. They had been beautiful. Sitting in warm water, soapy bubbles. Being clean. Going to parties. She didn't want to wake up from them, realizing they were mere dreams. The stench reminded her of the nightmare she was in. She opened her eyes to see Lily standing above her, straddling her face. Genitals again exposed. Lily was reaching for the roots dangling from the dirt ceiling. Patricia didn't move. She wanted to understand what Lily was doing.

Carefully the child twisted the tip of a dangling root and put it into her mouth quickly. She paused and looked around. Then she did it again. A piece fell and landed on Patricia's cheek causing her to flinch.

Lily gasped. "Don't tell the others. I am just so hungry."

"We all are." A booming voice came in through the door. It was Jimmy. He grabbed Lily roughly, and set her down on the floor.

"Lily. You must not pillage. Those belong to all of us. There is enough for all if we don't become selfish. Go now."

Lily let out a cry and ran from the room wailing loudly.

Patricia felt afraid again. Her brother looked so big in such a small room. He eyed Patricia suspiciously and approached her, looking into her eyes. Deep into her eyes as if he were looking through them and not at them.

Then, he reached over Patricia and took a whole root for himself raising his finger to his lips, as if it were a secret. "They are my favorite, too." He offered Patricia half.

Patricia shook her head, feeling her stomach grow sick again.

"Mother is waiting, and we mustn't keep Mother waiting. The Colony is waiting, too." He looked at her one last time as if warning her. Not trusting her.

Patricia sat up realizing she was half naked, and she shrunk back down, covering herself with her arms. Her head still spinning.

"We had to make sure you weren't carrying any tracking devices. Your clothes have been burned." He threw her a blanket and some undergarments. The texture of the blanket was strange.

"It's made of human hair. Not good enough for you?" he asked sharply. She wrapped it around her body quickly. "Human hair?"

"Yeah, we kill people and take their hair."

Patricia's eyes grew wide.

"I'm just kidding," he said. She wasn't sure whether to believe him. She didn't know what to believe. Like Father's world, who was there to trust and what is there to believe?

She followed him, her head still slightly throbbing, but better. Her bare feet on the dirt ground. Her stomach was empty and she thought of the dangling worms. She preferred to be hungry, for now. Her head itched again, and she saw a beetle in the thick hair wrapped around her. It dropped onto the ground and scurried into a dark corner.

They walked through more small rooms and tunnels. The walls were of dirt, as were the ceilings. In some areas she had to crouch down low. Corners were illuminated with small lights. LEDs, old technology. She recognized them from years before. Then, they came to a room with a circle of people sitting on a dirt floor. All eyes were on her.

"Welcome, Patricia. Sit down and join us. We were just about to have our morning tea. And it's time you learn our truth."

Patricia sat down cross legged. She tried to cover herself up the best she could. The hair blanket disgusted her, yet it was her only protection against the cavernous chill. The people in the room all watched her eyes. She noticed a man near Mother wearing her defunct OZ band and rubbing it as if it were a treasure. A thief? Who were these people?

Then it was quiet. Two people came in with trays of tin cans, broken Victorian tea cups. She was given a mug with an image of Santa Clause with the words "Ho, Ho, Ho, Be Good" The words made her shiver. She smelled the warm tea. "Drink!" Lily said. She had come up behind Patricia and sat down beside her. "It will make you human again."

"What is it?" "Silly, it's made with a beard!" Lily said, sipping her cup with her little finger raised.

"That is disgusting!" Patricia said and spilled her drink. Then she looked more closely and realized it was made with lichen, old man's beard, a drink even her father would take, an old family tradition.

"Friends, family, children. We are all together. And, we are only as strong as we are together. To think of ourselves as individuals is to behave selfishly. It is a way to lessen your power, our strength and our conviction." Mother started.

"Here, here" the group responded.

"Like the vast web of the mycelium, we grow slowly and spread. We are connected to the soil, the trees and the plants. And, one by one we will emerge from this soil where we grow, when the fruit of our belief is recognized and valued. The time is coming. And, it is the world's only hope."

"Here, here," the colony said together. "This is our truth."

Patricia's eyes grew wide. She looked at the people. "YOU are the Mushroom Colony?" she blurted out.

The silence seemingly grew thick. And, Mother looked at her, as if understanding what a moment of truth feels like. When you realize you have stepped out of the lightness of being and the truth of reality weighs heavily, like a crack in your own shell of existence. "Jonathon tried to explain to you," Mother said.

"Jonathon, my old boyfriend?"

Patricia also noticed something else. No one was sick. Filthy dirty, yes. Everyone had limbs, too, their own legs and arms. How many people had lost their limbs in her father's world, from wars to bad diets to insane mutilation, until her Father fixed the problems? She wondered about their medicine and their vaccines.

"How do take care of your sick people?" She asked. What do you do about the X1D virus when your people get it?" Everything Patricia touched she tried to wipe her hands clean, a habit she had acquired during The Great Collapse. But there was no clean place free of dirt. The idea of the surrounding deadly viruses and bacteria began to overwhelm her, like she could see them crawling on the dirt, on her body and their bodies, even in their breathing or laughing. Everywhere. It made her shudder even more. She pulled the hairy blanket around her tighter, but realized again what it was. Human hair! And, the people here didn't wash their hands before eating . . . and didn't seem to wash their hands for anything.

There was a momentary pause after she ignited the question. "How do you take care of your sick people, the ones with the viruses?"

Then, like a blast, the eruption of laughter began. She couldn't understand. Even the younger children were laughing.

"Sick? Ha!" Were they really sick in the head. They were crazy, She knew it. "I'm clearly NOT the crazy one." She tried to say in defense. "It's dangerous out there! People are dying every day from the new viruses! And YOU laugh at them? And look at how selfish you are by not even covering your faces and exposing your own germs!"

She was further disgusted by their lack of empathy. How many people had she seen die from the viruses. Women and even children! She began to remember the one day she swore on what she thought was her mother's proverbial grave that she would ALWAYS follow the highest protocol for cleanliness. Always. She would be the role model for responsible hygiene, how not to be selfish. Always washing hands, disinfecting her home. Even going through the highest process before sex at the salons. She remembered.

The Mother looked away from Patricia and spoke to Lily.

"Lily, you did your lessons well. Would you like to read to all?"

The child held a page with torn edges. Paper. Something that had disappeared. FAN banned it from society. Paper came from trees. A crime that needed to be stopped. Patricia looked at the paper as one would a product of greed. How the demand of paper had once destroyed forests. And, still, she marveled at the child reading from it, reading from something forbidden. And, the child could read.

"Yes, Mother. This is a poem in Iambic Pentameter by Alexander Pope. He wrote this in 1734," Lily went on.

"Know then thyself, presume not God to scan, The proper study of mankind is man. Plac'd on this isthmus of a middle state, A being darkly wise, and rudely great.

> With too much knowledge for the skeptics side,
> With too much weakness for the stoic's price,
> He hangs between, in doubt to act, or rest;
> In doubt to deem himself a god, or beast;
> In doubt his mind or body to prefer;
> Born but to die, and reasoning to err;
> Alike in ignorance, his reason such,
> Whether he thinks too little, or too much.
> Chaos of thought and passion, all confus'd,
>
> Created to half to rise, and half to fall;
> Great lord of all things, yet a prey to all;
> Sole judge of truth, in endless error hurl'd.
> The glory, jest and riddle of the world."

"Very good, Lily. In your own words, what does the poem mean?" Mother asked her.

"It means that men have been mucking it up for everyone for years. But, fortunately we girls have got it straight!"

The people burst into laughter. The Mother smiled. "Oh, Lily, you will blossom into a fine leader one day!" Lily gave Mother a hug.

"Friends," Mother began speaking. "I was once a teacher. I taught students about the ancient ways of ritual and respect. And I was spit on.

There was a clan, a wise forgotten people. A grandmother of this clan watched the development of modern civilization in a valley near their simple home. Before The Great Collapse. She said to her granddaughter: 'The people there are dangerous. They are all insane." They were unable to think for themselves and only followed greed and information that evil people spewed. People drove in cars using fossil fuels, before cars became the skeletal remains along highways of the world, as they are today. When people rushed believing their mundane actions were important, even if they convinced themselves they were educated, could read and write and operate in that modern society. And, vote for imaginary leaders."

"They were insane with stupidity, then and now, Mother," the brother burst out. He spit on the ground.

"We really will never know the full spiritual realm. For ourselves here, we value nature, this is sacred. This is what feeds both body, mind and spirit. We are in paradise. And we honor paradise. A gift here. And not in some faraway heaven.

A beetle walked into the circle.

"Lily?" Mother called out.

Lily ran to the circle and grabbed the beetle, sticking it into a box. The crowd watched and laughed at Lily admiringly. And, then there was silence.

"We have been cultivating a return to the spiritual realm, as nature has called us here. And we all had heard Her calling.

"Her?" Patricia said out loud.

"Patricia. You have lived in this Over World. Tell us how it is."

Everyone stared at Patricia again.

"First, I want to understand how you are all breathing the air and not poisoning each other with your viruses. How am I breathing it without dying?"

The colony laughed, like her question marked stupidity, ignorance.

"How much of the Over World do you understand?"

Patricia paused. She could make lies. She could weave a story like a web. She was indeed frightened, but also she felt there was no reason any more to tell any less than what she felt she knew. But, why did she have the impulse to defend her Father's world? This surprised even herself.

"Maybe there were untruths. But, the forests and oceans are healthier," she said. "The people were destroying it all. People are nothing but viruses themselves."

There was silence again. She caught sight of a large spider crawling into the circle. And, her brother smashed it with his fist.

"Jimmy. That was uncalled for."

"It bit me last night, Mother," he replied, cleaning his hand on the dirt.

Mother sighed. "Patricia. You came to the virgin forest to die. To take your own life. Why?"

"I have my own reasons for that," she answered.

"Your Father?"

Patricia suddenly felt like she wanted to protect him. But, why?

The Mother went on. "OZ, oxygen, air, was once there for all. Nobody questioned it. Until a profit could be made. That marked the beginning of FAN, Inc. your dear Father's company. When one takes more than what one needs, it begins a poisonous wave of greed. And his air is indeed poison."

The people nodded. "Here, here," they said.

"Anything beyond what we need is poison, Mother, whether its ambition, power, ego, food, fear or even Fruit Loops!" Lily shouted in.

"That's our Lily!" said Loopy.

Mother stopped to smile at Lily. "These are hard lessons. Our elders teach them to us. In the early 2000s, almost 50 years ago, we started to lose our elders. They were sent to homes away from us, with the idea they were impeding society's independence or ruining our economy, or that they needed their own security. They took with them wisdom, our history, our stories, our songs and many values. Our society became lost children while the schools became authoritarian, top down, brainwashing children about the world, making up stories to support greed and power, far beyond the imagination of anyone."

James stood up. He held Patricia's mask. "Patricia, your oxygen mask, which you believe keeps you alive, is designed to control you. The last bit is tainted with poison. If you don't change your supply quickly to a new supply, one with an antidote to cure, you become sick, like you did. It's a cycle that you entered once you become part of the system. The air outside is fine. Yes, polluted. But, the production of the oxygen that you rely on today is the cause of pollution today. Beyond your sacred virgin forests and oceans is another landscape of absolute destruction, worse than ever imagined. Just to ensure FAN and MOO's survival and control."

"What?" This was more confusing than anything Patricia could imagine.

"You have been deceived. Did Father tell you that?" he went on. "He's a liar!"

Patricia's head was no longer throbbing. It was spinning. "The banana slug?"

"Yes, an elixir, only after it eats a special mushroom. Lily is very adept in finding them. She has an eagle eye, we like to say. We remember the eagles of long ago, and we give them a voice, even if they no longer exist," Mother said looking down, as if remembering.

"But, I've seen the eagles." Patricia said. "And, Father has one."

The crowd again looked at her, shaking their heads, as if Patricia were insane or lying. At least that's how she felt.

Patricia thought back to licking the slug, and the thought made her stomach begin to sour. The heavy dust inside the chamber was suffocating. The human hair wrapped around her disgusting. The people filthy. She thought back to Father's Tower over the cities. There it seemed so clean, orderly and easy. She wanted to feel that way again. Why did she leave in the first place? Living like these people was unfit for an insect. No wonder spiders were running for their lives, she thought.

"The Technology Revolution was great, so everyone believed. Until it became the way. The only way, at least too many believed it then. Paper and pens were forbidden, in the name of protecting forests. People forgot how to write because they were told it was antiquated or even selfish to use tools that added to landfill. The computers were the knowledge keepers. Not the elders, not even the teachers. Information was lost, held up in vaults for only the leaders to access or distribute as they saw fit. Libraries closed, and the world became ignorant and hungry, completely dependent on MOO and FAN, Inc. Yes, surely FAN, Inc. saved people, but only on the corporation's terms. Everyone has an agenda. And, you are part of that agenda, Patricia."

"I've had enough. This is not about me." And, Patricia got up to walk away. "How do I get out of here?"

"Yes, Patricia, you are right. It's not just about you. It's about me, too." Patricia stopped and looked at Mother. "What do you mean?"

Mother stood up and walked into the circle to face Patricia. "Your father took our divorce to another level, one that no one has ever managed to accomplish. I am his prisoner, too, as we all are. My ideals are locked up in this Earth. And he's afraid. Patricia, because he is losing power. You are his last source of power. And my power is growing stronger."

"What power do you have, Mother? You're are living in a tomb, like the dead. You are crazier than those in Father's world," Patricia answered.

Mother looked to others in the room. "We feel the vibrations of the Earth. We feel the spirits move around us. The living planet has been ignored by too many for too long. You can't prove the spirits are here. You feel them when you understand them. You hear them whispering when you learn to listen. Your father has his way of seeing the world. Or controlling, but he doesn't listen. We are not in control. The spirits guide us, as long as you listen to them."

"You are all crazy." Patricia said. "I want to get out of here."

"Yes, Patricia, you will go back. You will have to go back to end this. And, that will be done in time. But not yet. Feast with us first." Mother began to walk away when Jimmy approached Mother.

"It's a risk sending her back, Mother. Let me go."

She eyed Jimmy for a moment, then looked at the circle of people and clapped her hands. "Everyone. Eat! Music! There are roots and berries. Nuts and delicate eggs. A tea made from redwood needles and mugwort for our dreams tonight. All from our small area in the woods. Know you have been the good stewards of this land. We take only what we need and respect it all. This is a good way to live. This is how our ancients lived, too, before the industrialists, the techies, the greed, the cancer began."

Mother then looked hard at James. "My son, I'm sacrificing my own daughter for the world. Her father sacrificed the world for his daughter. Tell me, who is the most fit parent?"

"Do you really think she can do what she needs to do?"

"I don't know, my son. I hope I'm not wrong. That is my burden to bear. It's incredulous to consider that I first believed the decision to leave your father would only affect my own two children. That was worry enough. But he took his rage out onto the world. How easy a drop can make a tsunami," she said and paused. "He promised me one thing. He would wait for me. He wants me to grovel back to him. And he has power. Much power. but he's losing it now. And that makes him even more dangerous."

"You and Father always favored Patricia."

"You both have different strengths, as well as different weaknesses, James. I love you both. And, I know your father does, too, in his own twisted way, though you are a danger to him the longer you are with me. I hope you understand that your own power is growing. And you must think more carefully now."

"I can take care of myself, Mother. You never believed in my strengths, ever. What do you think are my strengths?" Jimmy asked.

Mother became quiet. "Do you really need me to tell you? I'm sure your sister could share one of your strengths after you knocked her tooth out. And the way you punched your father in front of his colleagues when you were little."

"I see. I can hit well, and that's why I'm here. To help you." Jimmy stared at another spider crawling by. Mother saw it too and reached for his arm. This often settled Jimmy.

"The thing about you, Jimmy, is you can't see past your anger. You have a gift of seeing what others can't see. Injustices. You see truth on a deeper level than any of us. But instead of words you always use your fists. And, that hurts you more than anyone else. You have deep compassion, Jimmy. A big heart, maybe bigger than your soul can handle. I've done all that I can for you. All else is up to you. You have to become your own master."

Jimmy looked hard at Mother, as if he wanted to say something, but either couldn't or wouldn't. They were silent for a moment. Mother rubbed the soil with her fingertips. It was time to reveal a truth to Jimmy. Time to sift through the mixed messages and half truths. "We must let go of all the anger and fear and that includes you."

This provoked Jimmy. His anger began to rise and he hit the wall, shaking the dirt.

"Listen, in the FAN world you would be locked up or drugged up, Jimmy. Like all the other people who have special gifts or even half a brain, they don't fit in to your father's narrow world of what he, a single individual, wants. He calls them the mentally ill. Those who have a mind and living spirit of their own. If you can't fit into the system, or question the system, you are considered a deviant. They track you. They monitor you. They watch everything."

"I want to go in and face Father by myself. I can do it, Mother. I know him." Jimmy said. "I know all of Father's tricks."

The Mother looked curiously at Jimmy. "You haven't seen your father in over twenty five years, Jimmy. How would you really know?"

Jimmy looked away and bit his lip.

"Be patient, Jimmy. You will see your father in due time. Mother took a breath. "You know, our ancient societies were far beyond what the modern ones became. They honored the spiritual ones. The seers, those who could see beyond the narrowness of others. Those with the special gifts. Sometimes music or art. Most had vision. They could feel energy, energy of this planet. The spirits. They are the healers, Jimmy. Just like you. But, you are not listening just yet, with love and not anger.

Jimmy put his head down.

"Let them use your tongue, your mind. These spirits help us see the truth, through your music, Jimmy. The energy is flowing stronger now then ever before. Lily knows it. And, you know it. You feel it more than I do. That's why you're gifted. For us, the so called mentally ill, the spirited ones, the visionaries, we will be those who help save this world to reconnect the two worlds. We have to release the others in your Father's world. If they are slaughtered, there will be no hope to regain spiritual balance for centuries. Your father's system can't handle them. Too many are being born now, responding to the vibrations of the earth. The vibrations are strong than your father's world. It's our time."

"Maybe Father should get locked up." Jimmy said.

He lives with spite and ego. He did this because I left him. I feel responsible for his anger too. I feel a responsibility for the world. I can live underground with dirt for thirty years where I am free to make decisions, be who I am, speak. Love the way I want to love. I can't live in a world where one makes decisions for me. Silent forever. Shamed for being alive."

"And, how can you not be angry, Mother?"

I understand your father. I know his back story. His fears. His challenges. What I didn't realize was the depth of his ego and pride. Or love, for me, with a level of vindictiveness I could never imagine. The differences between the two of us became a battle ground for the world. And, our children are in between. But, I have hope, Jimmy. I have vision. I'm one of the crazy ones too, I suppose. Can you start to understand the burden I carry?"

"Just stop! Blah, blah, blah. I hate you talking. It's like polluting my head!" Jimmy, stomped on the spider and walked away.

Mother sat alone in the hollow of the dirt room. For the first time in thirty years she could feel the filth creep around her and the enormity of how she had lead the colony into this pit. Stuck. Until maybe now. There was hope. There were times she felt her belief had become a lie. A survival technique. Life had become all about survival. And, yet she had to portray hope. What else was there?

Mother closed her tired eyes and began to remember a different time. A dewy morning when walking through the woods and breathing fresh air seemed to be so normal. You'd never question it. Little Patricia held her hand. There were no dangers. It seemed. People were talking about melting ice caps and the world changing, but all that mattered was the changing of that chrysalis into butterfly. How they were both mesmerized by one on the fennel near the creek. They sat and watched it struggle for an hour and then emerge with the most beautiful black and yellow wings. The wind blew little Patricia's long hair while her big green eyes watched with wide joy. That look of wonder. Not with a smile, but something else. Something deeper. That expression when you connect with another life that speaks to you. It makes you go inward, and you feel something beyond anything you had felt before. Like electricity. A connection that lasts forever. Some call it love.

Chapter Four

"Time for blessings!" A voice called from the nearby room. The people had made a circle and were passing small sections of tree bark fashioned into platters, one by one, quietly. Carefully each person bowed to their plate and repeated "Thank you for life." They ate like children, using their hands. Solemnly.

Patricia watched. The chewing and gnawing became louder in the room. The plate came to her. She resisted the shriveled roots and insect parts, but did sip a drink made of pine needles and crushed berries with a flavor that burst in her mouth of memories long ago. Climbing trees and picking berries. Another life, it seemed. Another plate came by. The food was black, bread like looking.

"What is this?" She said before taking a piece.

The old man with dark almond eyes and gold loop earrings said, "You eat, and then we tell you." He grinned revealing black teeth. "My name is Loopy?" He grinned and his teeth were nearly black.

"We are not proud, Patricia," Another stranger said to her, taking a piece herself.

Patricia took a bite. It did look like bread. Dark bread. And she was hungry. She put a morsel into her mouth and found the taste satisfying. She chewed and swallowed.

"So what is it?" she asked revealing her own black teeth.

"Bread. Made with wild acorn flour and a seasonal addition." Loopy smiled again. Then he laughed loud and his tongue was black too.

Patricia stuck out her own tongue to look at it. "Why is my tongue black! What seasonal addition?" Patricia asked.

The man laughed and made a buzzing sound, gesturing with his hands.

"During certain moon phases, the East Lake flies come out in huge clouds. They are protein. We need protein. We like our black cakes." Mother said.

"You eat like rodents," and spat on the ground. Loopy laughed and took another bite.

"Actually we eat like humanity did before they ate like ravenous pigs and killed everything in sight." Jimmy said, taking a big piece for himself. "African tribes have been eating similar flies for centuries. Good enough for them so it's good enough for me.

"It's an honor to help keep the balance of nature, Patricia. We take only when it's right." the stranger said to Patricia. "It's enough."

Jimmy sat next to her. We don't eat like you ate in your perfect parfait MOO world, Patricia." Jimmy's teeth turned black too. And he spat black.

Lily came to Patricia. "I found you some clothing, Patricia, just like the good old days!"

Remnants, really. Patricia wanted to say. A t-shirt that had belonged to someone thirty years ago. She could tell. The shirt was from a rock concert. John Mayer, before he was arrested under MOO, along with many of the other musicians and artists. She never did learn what had happened to them.

"I remember his song. The one that got him into trouble with MOO." The old man with loop earrings spoke up again and half smiled at Patricia, as if he knew what she was thinking. That made her shiver.

"It was at a time when people made selfish music. Machine artists now make music. It's best for everyone. No self agendas. And, it's better for the brain. Scientists figured that out". She said. "It's called progress." She again was defending MOO and that surprised her. Being defensive of the placc she had run away from and prepared to take her own life.

"It was a good song. Very good song," the man said and he began to hum and sing. "Welcome to the real world, she said to me . . .r eal life and plan it out in black and white . . . I just found out there is no such thing as the real world. . . "

His black smile got bigger. His voice sounded so strange to Patricia. She wondered why he would make himself sound so stupid. He got up and started to dance and wiggle his body, leaving the room. "There is no such thing as a real world, just a lie you got to rise above . . ." he continued to sing, the words echoing in the long corridors.

Patricia turned to Jimmy. "Musicians are dangerous for society. They took so much power as individuals. Nobody should have that kind of power. Now all people are equal and there is peace." She could feel something crawl on her and she slapped her arm.

"Right, like dad. If there is peace, why did you run away?" Jimmy asked. He was whittling a stick into a sharp point.

"That's my business. Not yours."

She began to scratch frantically. "I feel like bugs are crawling all over me. Good God!"

"Bugs know where to find the rot," Jimmy said.

"I know you hate me. You've always hated me. Ever since we were little. Do you know it was a relief for me when you disappeared. I could finally live my life without you meddling in everything."

Jimmy eyed her. And, she wondered if he'd hit her. She wasn't scared though. She was daring him. Just like when they were children.

"You know why I disappeared, don't you?" He stopped whittling and eyed her hard.

Just then Lily came up to them. "Jimmy, let's take Patricia to the Moon tonight." Lily said with a quiet giggle.

"No."

"Jimmy. It's time. The vibrations are getting stronger. They tickle me. Almost make me hurt now. We don't have much more time." She whispered. "She needs to FEEL."

Jimmy was silent. Patricia felt another bug crawl on her. "Feel? I'm feeling enough right now." She scratched frantically. And stopped. "Vibrations?" She looked at Jimmy. "What is she talking about?" But he didn't answer the question. He kept staring at Lily as if she had broken a rule. But Lily smiled at him and he softened.

"Tonight. Tonight we will come for you, Patricia. Late tonight. And, Patricia, don't you dare fuck it up. Tell no one. We will go out there." he said. "To The Wildlands."

Who would Patricia tell? Who was a friend? Who was an enemy in this underground colony?

After the meal, the colony laid their hair mats on the floor of the Big Den. Loopy, the one with the black tongue, as Patricia had learned his name, thinking it had to do with his large looped earrings and uncanny personality, turned off the LED lamps one by one which made people rush quicker laying randomly on the ground. A few huddled together. Patricia sat on the outside of the circle. Lily plopped her mat next to Patricia, all the while caressing her bodiless doll's head carefully, like a protective little mother.

"At night the drones monitor the Wildlands," Lily said to Patricia, as if she could read Patricia's mind.

"We sleep together here so we won't get discovered at night. A redwood grove above shields us so we are safe. The trees tell us. Powerful nature is on our side."

"The trees tell you what?" Patricia asked.

Lily moved closer to Patricia and peered into her eyes, pausing.

"Everything," Lily whispered with eyes wide.

Like the words carried an electric charge, Patricia jolted her body away from Lily. The idea of being monitored, like the way MOO did every moment of every day sent a chill of terror into Patricia's body.

Lily giggled then crawled onto her matt fetus like with her doll.

The last light turned off and darkness crept deeper into Patricia's skin. The quiet became thicker. A cacophony of breathing, coughing and swallowing made discordant rhythms in the room.

"Just accept it." Lily said. "For now."

Again, how could Lily know what Patricia was thinking?

A figure walked through the room, humming of a song. It was Mother. Everyone in the room began to hum the song, quietly and gently. Then she remembered it. The River is flowing. Flowing and growing. The River is flowing. Back to the Sea. Mother Earth carry me. A child I will always be . . .

Mother put her hand on Patricia's shoulder and kissed the top of her head. We all sleep together here. Everyone, except for Jimmy. We accept that too." Mother said in the darkness.

"Where does he go?" Patricia asked.

"Likely another room to be alone. He needs his quiet time and privacy, just like when he was a child." Mother said and then left and disappeared into the darkness.

Patricia felt very alone in this filthy world of questions. Past and present were alike in this underground pit. Dark, disgusting and secretive. Patricia began to think of that song Loopy had been singing. It was familiar but it was so wrong. She thought of her father and the two of them seated in the Tower just last year. His Tower.

"Here, I'll show you something," Father had said. And Father walked to the big wall lined with a shelf of computer chips mounted like trophies. Patricia watched. He picked one up. "It's beautiful. Made from nature. Silicon. Sand. And the human brain. Ideas and information cast forever. The mind manipulates memories. It's not pure. But, these are pure. Better than books found in ancient monasteries. Those can fall apart. But, not the world of silicon."

He inserted a large chip into a hole in the wall and a door opened. "Come with me, Patricia." Inside was a chair. "Sit down. Maybe it's time for you to understand."

Patricia sat down and a heavy opaque glass door closed. It was vacant inside except for a chair sculpted of hardened sand.

"Sit inside and relax. I'll take your somewhere." Then he left her alone, closing the door behind him.

She had grown up in the Tower but she had never known of this room. There was nothing to see. Just blank walls. Grey walls. The air felt cold, lifeless.

Then it began. Music. A soft tone began to fill the room. Human made, she could tell. It sounded different then The MOO's music, that made by many digital voices. This came from one human. An egotistical human. Like one needing to show it's own peacock feathers, as her father had called it. This was dangerous music and it made her feel uncomfortable though it felt good. It tangled with her insides, stretching, relaxing, breathing into every cell of her body. She tried not to smile. She tried not to feel.

Light began to fill the space. Rods and swirls of it twisting into contorted shapes racing across the room. Three dimensional. Above her, next to her and around her. Faces. They began to shape into figures. An arm. A shoulder. A face. At first she didn't recognize them. Pictures formed, like old photos from the past world she'd seen in commercials. Blurry on the edges, out of focus. A thumb obscured one. Colors muted, not brilliant or sharp, like the images she was accustomed to, those that decorated the buildings and the world around her every day. But, still they drew her in.

A woman smiled, stretching her arm out to Patricia with a tray of cookies. That face. A mother. Her mother when she was young. A boy next to her. A brother. Her brother. He was smiling his devilish smile as she remembered him. Likely he had just hit her. Taken something from her. Did something bad like he always did. That's when she understood. This was her life. When she was a child. She sunk into the chair and watched. The music filling her. Another image. Father looked so young. He was smiling and making silly faces. There she was with a friend. An old school friend. Patricia wanted to reach out. Hug her mother. The one who had left her. But she didn't care. She wanted her. The tears began to flow.

Father entered the room quietly and stood next to Patricia then the images stopped and all was still. Father leaned over to Patricia and slapped her hard.

That same night they shared a meal together under the moon at the top of The Tower. A sumptuous dinner that he said was made just for her. A reward for understanding truth.

"You have to control emotions, Patricia. Then you'll become a great leader," he said that night.

Patricia had always been afraid of Father. But he was her father.

"Remember. She left you. I took care of you. I saved the world for you."

They ate in silence. No insects. It was a good meal even though she couldn't eat a bite.

She wondered if she could eat that meal now, as she curled into her hair mat. Then she conjured up her own future reality as she laid in the darkness. If they go outside, a drone could discover them as the drones always monitor The Wildlands at night. Then The MOO would come to rescue her and she'd explain everything. How crazy people lived underground like insects and believed they would save the world. Save the world from what? Father had already done that. He had been able to alter the climate change. Save the Wildlands, the oceans, the polar ice caps for future generations. These crazies belonged with the others – locked up so they could sing their selfish tunes with the other crazies. The song kept going around and around in her head until she finally dropped into a deep sleep.

Just hours later, though, Patricia woke up with a gasp, sitting straight up. It felt like a large beetle had rested on her shoulder biting her.

"Shhh," Lily said. It was just Lily's hand holding her shoulder, waking her. She was carrying a dim light on her head. "We go now. Follow me."

"Do I bring the flea bag?" she looked at her hair mat.

"No, leave it here." Jimmy answered. He was there too.

They walked single file, with Lily leading, along the dark corridors and then lifted a board that served as a ceiling, like a trap door. Dust spilled down onto Patricia and she coughed. Nobody apologized.

Patricia began to think about words she'd say to the authorities when they got caught. How she'd turn them all in. Even Lily. Maybe there was hope to turn Lily around into a proper child. A bath. School. She'd be good at the Terrestrial Museum that father owns, helping people learn about and connect to the natural world. Lily was a natural curiosity. Just like Ishi, once long ago. She'd serve humanity well one day. One day they could study her brain, learn how she can hear thoughts, or so it seemed. Patricia's mind began to wander wide. And, then she lost her footing and tripped.

"Shhh," Lily said.

"She's going to screw it up. Be careful." Jimmy said.

"Jimmy, let's remember, you were the one who always screwed things up. Every time we went somewhere with mom and day, you always threw the tantrums. Mom couldn't even handle you back then. I remember." Patricia said suddenly feeling bolder, more defensive. She didn't like Jimmy.

"Shut up." And, he turned around with wide eyes. Patricia thought his fist would fly, and then she felt really felt scared, seeing now that he was a full grown man and not the little annoying brother she had lived with long ago.

They crawled up and out of the trap door, entering a tight staircase, like one found in an ancient monastery. Dark and moist. There were no windows and the steps were carved small, so barely her foot could fit on each one.

"We're inside a soul." Lily said.

"A soul?" Patricia said.

"If you listen, you can hear it. Feel it."

They kept climbing higher and higher until they reached the top. Patricia was nearly out of breath and legs ached. Still, there were no windows. The smell was of moist fungus. She wondered what could be behind the door. It was as if they were climbing the heights of her father's Tower.

Then they stopped. "Now we mustn't even whisper. We talk with our eyes until we reach the other side." Lily said.

Jimmy pushed the wooden door open. And, there before them was a long, thick tree branch, in a canopy of a redwood tree, three hundred feet high above the ground.

"My God," Patricia said as she looked down.

"No talking," James said with his wild eyes again.

James gave Patricia a rope and harness to put around her waist. And, then he put one around his own. But not Lily. She climbed into Jimmy's arms. And, then they swung to the branch of another tree. Patricia was mesmerized by this. Just like Tarzan, she thought and almost laughed. But, she was left alone on the branch, understanding the fact they were now like flying squirrels instead of living amongst the insects. But before she could complete that thought, she was jerked off her feet and her body swung across the open space to the limb of another tree. She gasped and nearly crashed into her brother's arms. Lily was sitting on the branch dangling her feet. "Jesus Christ" Patricia said. "What the fuck?"

"They are coming. Quiet."

Patricia looked down to see three hovering drones half way between them and the ground. Lily kept her finger to her lips. Patricia watched, curious. She had forgotten it was a chance to forget this mushroom world and return to her former life. In the next moment, the drones were gone.

"They'll be back. For now we can talk. Only if we need to."

Patricia couldn't deny the drones set her in a sort of fear. Panic. It didn't seem right. As if drones were not prone to reason. Or compassion.

They sat in the tree listening to the forest. The branches swayed slightly and wind whispered through the needles. Both Lily and Jimmy had their eyes closed and sat still on the edge of the branch.

Patricia felt annoyed. Why were they just sitting there? "Are we going somewhere or what?" Patricia finally said.

"Listen. The trees are talking," Lily said

These were The Wildlands, Patricia thought. Wild. Crazy wild. Everyone. Everything.

"It's just a tree," Patricia said.

"Jimmy turned to her with his contemptuous eyes. It's a universe if you stop and listen. It carries a spirit. Listen to the spirits. They are talking. You can feel them, only if you listen."

Patricia listened. She was itchy and couldn't hold still. She heard something rustle on the branch. So she scooted closer to the rustling sound. "I hear it," she said. And, she reached over into a pile of needles that collected in the arm of the tree. Something was moving in it. A salamander. A black salamander sitting in the thick of the needles.

"It's not the trees talking. It's a salamander. You guys have been spending too much time in thar' hills," she said, with a half laugh.

She picked up the salamander, one she remembered from the Terrestrial Museum. They live their entire lives in the redwood canopies. A whole world to themselves, never touching the ground. Now, from insects, to flying squirrels to amphibians, she thought. She held it close to her eyes, wondering if it might have some disease as many of them did when they were brought to the Terrestrial World. Her father helped save them for the public good, public education.

Her thoughts went deeper. And she began to remember.

A witch's cauldron. Alive with termites. That's how she remembered the hallowed dead tree trunk that day where she had played with sticks and leaves. Then she climbed into it and she stepped on a dragon the size of her arm. She screamed loudly. "Mom." and cried. Mother was there in a heartbeat, two racing heart beats colliding in a hug. "What is it, my dear?"

Mother peered into the trunk just like Patricia, the curious child. "A salamander! It's huge! Beautiful! Do you want to hold it?"

Mother lifted it out of the log carefully and placed it in Patricia's little hands like a gift. They marveled at his exotic beauty. It's head, it's web feet. It's speckled smooth skin.

Father walked toward them, carrying two year old baby Jimmy on his shoulders. "I'm disappointed you don't know your salamanders. That's a Giant California

Salamander," he looked at mother the way he did
sometimes. He always knew more than her, or so it seemed.

"Can I bring it home?" Patricia had asked.

*It's a native species, Patricia." Then he turned to
mother. "What are you teaching her? She's eight years
old and still asking these questions? I thought you were
a nature teacher. Clearly you need help with your job."*

*Then he turned to Patricia. "It's selfish of you, Patricia.
Keep the wild in the wild," he said sternly and took the
salamander out of her hands.*

Patricia unthinkingly released her grip on the
salamander from the redwood canopy top and it
dropped, plummeting to the ground. She didn't mean
to drop it. She gasped.

"Don't Lily!" Jimmy said. But it was too late.

Lily jumped to the next branch and scrambled down
the tree one limb after another until she could go no
further. Then, she grabbed a rope and swung down
to the ground, scrambling toward the salamander.

"Lily!" Jimmy shouted. They are coming!

Lily picked up the salamander and examined it.

"Lily come back!" Jimmy shouted.

Patricia grew nervous. And, suddenly she felt the
panic and wanted Lily safe.

"You fucked this up," Jimmy said to Patricia.

"He's okay, Jimmy. He's a tough one!" And, then
Lily turned and ran into the nearby grove of giant
ferns, disappearing from sight.

"They are coming. Don't say a word," Jimmy said to Patricia.

"How do you know they are coming?" Patricia said.

"The trees are talking. The ferns told Lily where to hide."

Patricia watched her brother. He really believed this shit. The talking trees.

"So, what language do your trees speak?" Patricia asked, almost laughing at the absurdity of it all, hiding from drones and listening to talking trees, while living like an insect underground. "Your world is truly mad." she said.

"Quiet!" Jimmy said.

The drones did come. Vibrating disks that moved slowly. Humming. They hovered for what seemed like a longer time near the ground below them. Patricia wondered if they could sense Lily amidst the giant ferns. These were her father's drones. What were they after? Why were they coming here? Were they looking for her? She held her wrist to see the scar from the cut she made, a crime of removing her chip, the old chip, not the new one that was impossible to remove, that had become the legal implanted ID on the island. Father had said he trusted her.

Then the drones left. There was silence. Lily came running out of the ferns and began twirling below, dancing and giggling.

"Come quick, Lily!" Jimmy dropped the rope down to Lily and pulled her up. Lily stood facing Patricia. She had a frond sticking out of her hair like a feather. Gold patterns covered Lily's dark clothes. They shimmered in the moonlight.

"Miss Patricia. Please put this salamander back home and apologize," Lily said.

"I'm sorry?" Patricia said sarcastically.

"Say it like you mean it," Lily said again.

"I'm sorry." Patricia said with more compassion. Jimmy was staring at her, like he'd hit her to make her say sorry. But, he didn't hit.

"They won't come back for a while," Lily said.

Patricia kept looking at Lily's clothes. "What is that on you?"

"Gifts from the ferns." she smiled. "The Goldback Ferns."

"Jimmy, the Sword Fern gave me this, to help protect me." Lily giggled again and showed him a frond.

"The ferns talk to you, Lily?" Patricia asked.

"Oh, yes," she giggled. "They tickle me too! Do you want to be tickled by them?" And Lily took the fern out of her hair and with it tickled Patricia's face, giggling."

Patricia didn't giggle, though. "No thank you, please."

They were quiet again.

"So, what are your trees saying now?" Patricia asked.

"The trees speak a language only if you listen. And, you haven't been listening well enough. We are not the crazy ones. Ask Father. He is the one who doesn't listen and you listen to him." Jimmy said.

"What do you mean?"

Lily looked at Jimmy. "Your mother can explain better. Now we sit and watch."

They sat there high on the branch. A large orange moon rose from behind a mountain. Shadows emerged on the ground, those of trees, giant ferns and shrubs that surrounded them. A great owl flew between the trees and hoots were heard echoing through the forest. The wind had even settled, creating a thick silence and yet subtle sounds were beginning to grow louder. A rustling insect, the dropping of a pine cone. A rodent running in a tree. Patricia became mesmerized. Even the salamander next to her seemed comforted in its nest.

"Do you hear the music?" Lily asked.

"Music? I thought I was listening for the talking trees?"

Lily giggled like a demon-child again. "The vibrations from all the life around us. The moving universe." Lily pointed to stars in the sky. "It's beautiful tonight isn't it, Jimmy."

"I don't hear anything," Patricia said again.

"Jimmy, why don't you play with it," Lily giggled. "Your sister is not a spirited one."

Jimmy lifted a small flute, the size of a large acorn and blew into it. A sound with edge emerged. A simple short melody began, repeating, echoing across the valley, as if nature were listening. The shadows of the moonlight swayed and danced. Like all that was alive was connecting to the sound. Patricia began to feel something deep inside her. Stirring. Mixing. A rhythm.

A calm. Connecting. A feeling she had not felt in many years. Why? It's a simple sound coming from a nut. Her brother. An Acorn. A primitive sound. Why should it be affecting her so much? It was like tingling her blood. Making her whole body feel different. She tried to stop the feeling. It was uncomfortable. As if it were illegal.

"Music comes from the universe. It's the spirited ones who can feel the vibrations the most. We are the spirited ones at the Mushroom Colony, me and Jimmy. The colony respects us. And we help them. We hear the vibrations of the Great Mother. They mix with our soul. That's how we make music for people like you Patricia, who don't have our gift."

Was that an insult? Patricia wondered.

"People in your world don't understand humans anymore. Only machines. Why don't you have music in your world, Patricia?"

"We do! We have music everywhere. You don't know my world. People care about one another there. And, we don't have to hide." Again she found herself protecting what she had run from. Why?

"Really?" Lily giggled.

Jimmy laughed too as if it were a secret joke. Then Lily got serious.

"I didn't say it right. Why don't you have music in your world that's made by people?"

"Too many machines kill Spirit. You listen to dead music," Jimmy said.

"Oh." Patricia now understood the question. Yes, we have scientists who have learned to make music that affects certain parts of our brain in order to give pleasure. The cortex, receptors in the hyppocampus and neurons all affect the way we experience something. The feelings you have right now are all a result of reactions in your brain. You're being manipulated and you don't even know why or how. Who is the stupid one?"

"We are the messengers of nature. Our souls talk to the unspirited ones, those who refuse to listen. We help save them. Connect them to nature. Their own nature. They are the same." Lily giggled like a demon child. Or, an angel. Patricia couldn't discern.

"You can't lock us up. Or, drug us up. The vibrations just get stronger and stronger. Then, it's too late." Lily frowned and then moved deeper into the shadows of the tree and sat by herself.

They were such curious words coming from a child or propaganda she's been trained to say. Who was this child? Patricia thought.

Jimmy continued to play music now with a simple reed on his lips. How did he do it? It was a beautiful sound still. She thought about her brain and what the scientists could tell her about the neurons, which part was being triggered and how. It's important not to let the music get you emotional because that's how you lose control. Never lose control and never be manipulated emotionally by music. It's not different than propaganda, she remembered learning in school. Be strong. Always be strong. Resist.

She looked up to the vast stars above, the moonlight shimmering through the valley. She grew restless as she listened. She tried to listen without those voices inside her telling her how to think. She thought of her Father's world. The problems with the mentally ill. The ones father wanted to kill.

"We can't hold out anymore. The mentally ill and elderly are beginning to dominate society. They're filling up the institutions," Father said at the board meeting. As always, he sat at the head of the table. In his chair, one made of redwood, recycled, the last one ever robbed from The Wildlands.

"We serve humanity and the natural world on a top level. Helping individuals cope with those who can't help themselves. If you can't handle society, then we can't handle you. That's my motto. Responsibility by all. Otherwise, you don't deserve The Island.

Cyrus, her father's top advisor, spoke. "We have tried. MOO's medical team, therapists, drug companies have all spent enormous resources to train these people. Why, many can't even push buttons when you ask them to! They're incapable of the most minimal tasks. We've tried. Over and over again. Many fly into rages, become dangerous. They just sit in a stupor like they're dead. What use are they?" His slender white fingers tapped the table with a rhythm as he talked.

"We could release them to The Wildlands," one said. "Let them figure out their own lives."

Father pounded the table. "No! Nobody goes out to The Wildlands. Off limits." He paused, collecting himself, touching his heart. "The Wildlands are still not safe. The disease from years of pollution is out there. We need to let it heal." Father said. "We can't do that to the people of The Island who have worked hard to help restore balance."

Patricia walked in.

"I can't do that to my daughter." he smiles. "Hello Patricia."

One murmurs to another. "I've heard many of the people talk about a dangerous mushroom colony. I don't know where they're getting this information. It's nothing that we've distributed. And I've not seen any unnatural imbalances, other than a turkey mushrooms, but those can be found right here at the table at times."

Father hears this. Then looks at Patricia. She picks up a strawberry from the table. "Strawberries. This must be a special occasion." Patricia says. "Father, here's the report you wanted."

"It's the annual meeting, Patricia." Father scans it and sets it down quietly on the table.

"Patricia, why don't you join us now. We were just talking about an important matter. Maybe it's time you begin to understand the gravity of the issue. My daughter has tried helping one of the people in question at the Terrestrial World. Maybe now, Patricia, you will gain an understanding why we had to send Jonathan away."

Patricia looks at the group. Father continues. "Let me tell you about Jonathan." Patricia doesn't say a word. "You see, my beautiful daughter likes to teach others at the Terrestrial World the beauty of nature. I might add my daughter has learned well from The Island

Community. She tried to help one who was clearly mentally ill. He was on the XR7 medication, even had his label on to ensure others understood his condition. In order to instill compassion. My daughter left him feeding the ambassador salamanders, the ones FAN, Inc. saved. Jonathon had stuffed several in his pockets ready to kill these magnificent creatures.

"Father, he said he was going to release them."

"It's the same as killing them, Patricia. They were under my care. I say when they are ready."

Patricia looked down.

"This man Jonathan was merely asked to adjust the temperatures. Push buttons, as you like to say, Cyrus. But, this man clearly had an agenda. When he was caught, he flew into a rage, crashing one of the aquariums, nearly killing some of our most important fish and reptiles. He kept saying he could feel what the animals felt. He could hear them talking. They would prefer to be dead. Well, this man nearly did it to himself as well as to a few of our good men at MOO. His damage cost considerably. As is always the case."

The men grumbled at the table.

"See, Patricia. We can't trust these people." Father paused and then stood up, pacing the floor as he looked at the report Patricia had given him. "The problem, gentlemen, is that according to this report and analysis of this past year, the numbers are rising. We can't figure out how to test for this type of mental illness, but according to the information that we collected from across The Island, the number of those who can't perform are enormous.

That's good news for you, Cyrus, but not for a healthy Island State. Our institutions with the old people too are overcrowded. We can't take more on.

"We could expand The Island." another said.

"Yes, like Manifest Destiny, Franklin? That is exactly the attitude that began to rot our world until we could barely survive in it. We have achieved balance. Reversed melting icecaps, acidic oceans and toxic blight across the lands. Our world is rejuvenating. Be proud of the sacrifices we've made.That which should be wild is wild. We will not go back to the past. We need to be disciplined. It's our problem therefore we should solve our problem."

"What do you suggest?" Franklin, the other advisor asked.

"If I may say so, we could test more drugs and increase distribution." Jeremy spoke up. "Our neuroscientists have uncovered incredible new information based on recent research that isolates the genome causing deficiency of micro processing skills. If we could expand that research I feel confident we could generate medication for a higher level distribution. It helps people. It helps the economy. It's our way of helping humanity on The Island, sir."

"Thank you, Jeremy. We value your contribution." Father said. "People on the street say if you are not taking medication, than you are not being honest with your mental issues. Everyone has issues. You've done remarkable work, Cyrus, Jeremy and the rest of the MOO and FAN members. Helping everybody. People are beginning to recognize they must do their part and make sacrifices to

keep the balance of our society. Only then can they take steps to control deficient habits."

"Thank you, sir. That means a lot to me." Cyrus said. "It's been my life work, you know."

"You're like a son to me, Cyrus." Father paused and looked out the window to the white washed buildings below. He liked this view, the one that showed how well architecture can mirror nature. Honeycomb designs, efficient energy living. The air appeared clean. He saw a child running in the street noting how healthy the small child ran with his OZ mask. He smiled then turned back to the table.

"Do you see, Patricia, the leadership in this room?" Father said. "People in this room are like family. They do care."

He then looked at the gentlemen in the room. "My Patricia sometimes questions whether or not we care. That is why I have her sitting here with us today. She is beginning to understand. Aren't you, Patricia?"

Father touched his heart.

"Are you okay, sir?"

"Yes, it was just an electric pulse. Where's my assistant, damn it?" Father sat down and looked at the monitor on his wrist.

"Patricia, why don't you read the first lines of the report and share with the leaders."

"Okay." Patricia felt important. She liked that.

"Can I ask a question first", Cyrus spoke up. "I don't think we solved the issue about the mentally ill, with respect sir.

"I ask you a simple question." Father said. "Tell me this, with the extreme cases. The ones in the Solace Chambers. The ones who scream when they get close to our systems. The real crazies. Would we miss them? Would anyone miss them?"

The board was quiet.

"Father, your assistant is here." Patricia said. A small woman walked into the room. Her head was shaved. Her oxygen mask was still on even though the air in the building was fine.

"Delany, you're being neglectful and irresponsible. Look at the time. Many thoughtful people take extra care in ensuring people like you have the medication to take. It's your responsibility to uphold that kindness."

"Yes, sir."

She started to tear up.

"You are getting emotional. I'm disappointed. You'll need to remedy that. I can't deal with that kind of pettiness. Or, I'll need to find new help."

"I'm sorry sir. My computer crashed with my schedule so I couldn't figure out when . . ."

"No excuses, Delany" Father said. And, he looked at the men. "Don't start blaming technology for your own lack of reason and responsibilities."

"Yes, sir."

Delany started to leave.

"Wait, Delany. Come here." She did. He picked up her young hand. "Look at this beautiful work of nature. A hand. A beautiful hand. That which binds each of us together. He touched her hand. A stroke. Delany reacted

*stepping back. "I like your hand, Delany." He smiled at
her but she didn't smile back. "You are excused now."*

Patricia watched Delany's hand and then looked at
her own, a memory or was it a story she had read came
to mind, of someone touching her hand that way.

"It's amazing to me how you can create all these tools
for people, and they still can't get it right. Our technology.
Our medicine. And, still people complain. The point is
you can do everything for people but if they can't do it
themselves, even push a dam button, it's time to withdraw
that help. Have I made myself clear?"

"All we can do it try, right Counsel?" Cyrus responded.

"Yes." Father paused again. "Though, leaders, I hope
you did notice that my assistant was wearing her oxygen
mask. You've done well with the design. People now prefer
to wear them than not wear them. They have become a
fashionable statement, haven't they? I see Delaney likes
the most sophisticated one."

Father took his medication. "Thank you again, MOO,
FAN and Island Leaders, for your contribution to our
Island Societies and to The Wildlands. We'll visit the
report next week. It can wait. Enough for today."

The leaders left the room but Father and Patricia
stayed at the table.

"What were you talking about?" Patricia asked Father.
"The mentally ill. You asked whether or not if they would
be missed."

Patricia watched Lily through the moonlight play with ferns she had collected. At the moment she hated Lily. She hated how she played, so stupid. Making up stories that aren't true. "Stick with the facts" father would always shout along with her school teachers. "She's too happy. Knock her down to understand reality." The words continued to come but they were also mingling with the music Jimmy continued to play.

"Time to go!" Lily said.

And with that, the three climbed down the tree with the use of vines. "Where are we going?" Patricia asked.

Once at the bottom, on the forest floor, Lily stuffed the ferns into her shirt like wings and held others in her hand. She twirled around. "Thank you trees! I'm a peacock, a peacock. . . and I can see everything with eyes all over me!"

These words unsettled Patricia, like The MOO world, always being watched. "Don't say that," Patricia blurted out.

"Oh, we are being watched, though. See?" Lily turned over the fern to the little round spores. "I'll prove it!" Lily blew the ferns toward the moonlight, and like little fairies, the spores drifted off into the air. "Goodbye, spirits! Keep us safe!"

"What are you talking about? Those are just reproductive organs of a plant that doesn't talk. They see and feel nothing." Patricia was growing weary of Lily.

"Oh, no!" Lily took offense. They are part of the spirit world and they are always watching out for those of us who are good."

This sounded like MOO and Patricia began again to grow uneasy of this colony. "Right, just like Santa Clause."

Lily burst out laughing. "That's a good one! Can you believe all those kids who believed a fat man lived in The Northpole!" She giggled more. "He couldn't even take care of the melting snow in the North Pole so how could he ever manage getting down a chimney!"

Patricia almost laughed at Lily's comment but she still felt defensive. Why? Then another thought came to her. The peacock. The peacock. She looked at Lily who had tied the fronds with a blade of grass and crafted herself with what looked like a peacock tail. Patricia had been a peacock, as a child. Her mother had made her that costume, one of the most beautiful and sacred birds, her mother had said with a kiss on the forehead.

"I have a present for you," Lily said to Patricia, though Patricia was still in that dream world, remembering something from long a go, a distant memory, when she wore those feathers with joy.

"Hold still now. It's a gift from the fern spirits. I am the messenger." Lily placed a fern on Patricia's face. "Close your eyes." Lily pushed the fern firmly against her face with her small hands. Her breath close to hers. A gentleness and tenderness she hadn't felt in so many years. Maybe decades. Lily began to twist Patricia's long hair and it felt so good to Patricia, being gently touched by a child. Listening to her humming, reminding Patricia of her own childhood that had stopped so fast.

"Almost done. I just have a few more things to do." Lily looked at Patricia's face and smiled. Then she touched her lips.

"What are you doing?" Patricia responded.

"It's a blessing. You'll see. Let's go home."

Jimmy shouted from the valley below. She hadn't noticed he had wandered away.

When they returned to the underground den, candles were lit. Many were still asleep. Some were waking up.

"Here, here!" Lily announced skipping into the room. Loopy turned and smiled his half toothless grin. "A queen has come!" He bowed to Patricia and winked at Lily.

His teeth were still black. "Go look at yourself in the mirror. Welcome to the crazy club!" he said to Patricia.

Lily pitched in fast. "It's the Queen of the Forest, Loopy. Show some respect."

"Oh, excuse me!" Loopy bowed deeply again to Patricia.

"What did you do to me, Lily?"

Patricia walked toward a cracked mirror leaning against the dirt wall. There were gold sparkles all over her face. Her hair was adorned with flowers and ferns. She actually looked almost beautiful, a natural beauty, even with the hair blanket around her. She hadn't seen herself since MOO days with makeup and clean clothes. She stood in wonder, being reminded of another childhood memory. There was a crack in the mirror. And like a crack in her own hardened spirit, a flood of tears began to wash down Patricia's face. She felt as if her whole body was cracking and fell onto her knees, staring at herself. Who is she?

Mother walked into the room and smiled. "The time is coming," Mother said. "Lily, go check on the cook to see if we have a proper meal and the food needed for the day. Jimmy is in there with the harvest of fiddle heads and berries."

Lily clasped her hands and started to sing. "She's feeling! She's feeling, Mother! We cracked her soul, made her bleed and now she's back to feeling!" Lily sang the words loudly, skipping away.

Patricia was still on her knees looking at herself. Mother put a blanket over her. "I've kept this for you. Maybe you remember." It was a quilt made by her grandmother, a soft cotton made with images of giraffes, plants and flowers. It smelled fresh, like maybe rosemary or a hint of bay.

"Go rest. You've had a long night in The Wildlands. Tonight we have a special meal. We will need your help later today," Mother said to Patricia.

What was happening to Patricia? Why all these feelings? She couldn't even describe them all twisting and writhing inside her Then, in the mirror, beyond her reflection, she saw a dark figure crumpled in a blanket staring back at her. A woman. Dirty. Long hair and penetrating eyes. Blue eyes. Eyes that she's seen before. Or has she gone insane? The figure pulled a blanket over itself more, as if hiding from Patricia. Patricia was drawn to this person who suddenly screamed out, "Go away. I hate you. All of you!"

That voice. Patricia walked closer. "Wait, Patricia," Mother said. But Patricia didn't wait.

That voice. She's heard it before. Those eyes. Those blue eyes. "Who are you?" The figure took off the dark cape and looked up at Patricia. Patricia let out a scream so loud that the walls shook with dirt.

"The witch! What the fuck is SHE doing here!"

Chapter Five

Patricia remembers the day. That feeling. That feeling her mother had always said to follow. That gut feeling that will tell you of danger and run. She didn't run though. Patricia remembers. She remembers.

"She's a beautiful girl", the girlfriend said to Father. His new girlfriend who had come so quickly, seemingly overnight. Yes, she was beautiful. Long red hair. A former actress who knew how to play her role well. She touched him along his arm and it tingled his spine. His body began to throb. She had told him love is connected spiritually between the heart and the libido. "It ties us to the universe," and he wanted to believe her. He wanted to feel complete, whole, and understood for the first time in his life. This was all supposed to happen. Like a boy with his mother, he felt safe with this woman who called herself Asura. And all the friends she brought

into his life, into his home. They felt like family, like they understood him.

"It's her time," Asura spoke, looking at Patricia with the budding nipples. Patricia couldn't hear what they were saying. She didn't trust Asura. She didn't like how she came into her father's life so fast after her mother left. She didn't like how bossy she was telling her what to believe and what to do.

"Patricia will love you, Dear. You are helping her connect to her spirituality even if she doesn't know it yet. The community will embrace you understanding that it's a difficult path for a father to choose what is higher and good, not just for her but for the entire community. You'll be honored." Asura took his hand and squeezed it tight. Love. He could feel it. He loved to be loved. He wanted to be loved.

She knew too the power she had on him. And she knew she had to act fast, just like the spiders he was fond of. She smiled feeling how good her life was becoming. Understanding that her failures as an actress were merely a journey to this point in her life to inherit well and finally be comfortable in life, a reward for all her efforts. For all to revere her. Her beauty, voice and sexuality. She would be honored for this not just from her own community but perhaps the world.

She also knew her idea for Patricia would tie them together and be more complete. The mother would have less power. She liked that. She knew how to position herself, just as she would do on the stage. To lay her mark.

"It'll make us more like a family. A tighter family." she kissed his cheek.

Father loved her voice too. Seductive, but gentle. A true woman. Not like his former wife who always yelled and spoke down to him. She didn't understand love and compassion. Now he understood. Love was the universe. He was love and he liked it when she told him that.

"As her father, wouldn't it be wonderful to be there with her for her first time. To welcome her to womanhood, the divine feminine essence?" said whispering to him and nibbling his ear.

He trusted her. How couldn't he? She was beautiful and could look into his eyes bewitchingly. Pure love and bodily essence. It was one in the same. The orgasms and the all night cuddling. And she accepted him for all that he was.

Yet there was a hint of reluctance in his eyes. This was his daughter after all. His only daughter.

"You. You are her father. It's proper to be the one. She looked at him straight in the eyes unflinchingly. I will be here with you. She trusts you. You will not hurt her. It's the proper thing to do," she said. "It'll be a ritual with flowers and music. Incense too. We'll have a full meal together. Then she can become a woman and know how to be treated with love all her life."

Father looked at Patricia who was in the next room reading a book. She looked so much like her Mother. He hated her for leaving him.

"You two will unite on a level unlike any other. Do you understand? It's pure, Charles. We'll do this all together."

She put her hand on his shoulder to reassure him. There was a glint of concern in his eye. She didn't like that but she wasn't worried, never worried. She knew how to wipe it away. Her smile. A smile she knew he liked.

"Good. Charles. You are such a good father. You will lead other fathers. People will see our way."

She kissed him on the lips. His dry lips. She licked them like a wound. She knew the prowess of a cat. She knew she'd have to strike when it was time too.

"After, you and me will have Tantra and fly into ecstasy, together. The plan of the universe. We're all one. We're all divine. This time we take it to a higher level. Three of us for you.

It had been so hard with his wife, laying in bed. She moved away from him toward the last years, sleeping on the edge of the bed and not wanting him to touch her. How did this goddess girlfriend know what he wanted? She knew everything he wanted, so it seemed. They spoke the same language. It fit so perfectly together. It was the universal design. She even told him this.

He sloughed off his worries. She was beautiful. He could trust her. A pure goddess. She had gotten him this far in life, nurturing him after his wife left him.

Asura grabbed his hand and held it to her heart. Feel me throb. My heart. She hugged him, heart to heart. You and I have been meant for each other. I've waited long for you.

"I'm a woman. Divine feminism. I understand these things, dear. Remember, your wife was an angry woman. She didn't understand love. And surely she didn't understand her place."

"You know everything," he said.

She smiled then smiled again.

"The night of the new moon," Asura said to the father. "Next week. We'll have a feast just like the Romans or the Egyptians."

Rome. Egypt. The universe played in a divine way. He felt so connected to that higher place. It made his dick hard. Her hand rested there.

"Hi Patricia," Asura said. "Your father has something for you. I'm honored to be the messenger. It's beautiful that he loves you very much. I'm glad we're friends."

Patricia looked away. "I never said we were friends."

"Hmmm. I view you as a daughter, you know. A daughter I never had. But the universe brought us together."

"You're not my mother."

Asura shot a glance across the room and bit her lip. She looked again at Patricia Her lips curved to form a crescent moon.

"See the beautiful dress your father bought you?" Asura said as she held it up against her own body.

"He didn't choose it. You did."

"I know you don't understand these things yet. Trust me, Patricia."

"Why would I trust you?" Patricia didn't trust. She got that funny feeling in her stomach when Asura was around.

"Tonight is a full moon. Do you know what that means? It's a moon for you. To be like a woman. To show your womanhood. It's your night to have pleasure for the first time."

Patricia watched her. That feeling deepened in her belly.

"Pleasure?"

"Yes, it's your divine right to have pleasure. Would you like that? We'll eat together and then we will all celebrate you."

"I don't want to be celebrated. I want to stay in my room".

That crescent moon appeared again. Patricia could feel darkness like the black sky.

"Your father will come to get you when it's time. You want to make your father happy, don't you?" Asura said. She licked her lips again and the crescent moon appeared. Black like a witches cat.

Patricia did want to make her father happy. She missed her mother so much. Why did she leave her and her brother in such a mess? She felt so alone. She looked at the dress laying next to her on the bed. She hated frilly things. Asura's Goddess stuff was disgusting. What did her mother say? Narcissism.

That night Father knocked on the door. "Hi sweetheart. Can I come in?"

"Sure." she said.

"How are you feeling?"

"Okay."

"Asura has put a lot of work into this, you know. La Sorc will be here tonight as well. You met him on Christmas. Do you remember the chocolate he brought? He's done years worth of coaching, you understand. Patricia, it took me a long time to understand love. I had so much anger in me before. La Sorc and Asura have taught me deeply about compassion and how I fit

in to this universe. We are all one, you understand. This community is our family now. I think after tonight you'd make Asura feel very good about calling her mother. And tonight you'll bring greatness to our home".

"Greatness? Dad, you're weird," Patricia said.

"You listened to your mother too much. There are things about the universe she didn't understand that I have learned. She was so filled with hate and anger, you know. But, I have compassion for her as you should too. She didn't understand gifts we're given in life. Asura does and I trust her because of that. You see, she taught me. We chant for your mother every night, Patricia. We care for her, too. See how much compassion Asura has?"

Father touched Patricia's hair. "I'd like to see you beautiful, Patricia. Just like your mother. She was beautiful, you know." He turned before looking back at her. "Be your mother tonight. For me." Father left the room and closed the door.

Patricia was alone. She loved her father. She hated herself. Every little bit of herself. Ugly. She looked at herself in the mirror. Long dark hair with rats. She liked the rats. They were honest. The tangles. That what this was all about. How to untangle the hair. It would hurt and she didn't know how to start combing. It all made her want to throw up. God, she wanted her mother.

"Always listen to your gut, Patricia," mother had said one afternoon. Patricia remembered that moment well. Mother grabbed her hands and looked at her hard in the eyes. "Always follow your gut, even if it means going against your mother and father. Do you understand me?

I give you permission. Do what YOU feel is right. Run, if you have to. Run like fucking hell, if you have to."

Was this a time to run? Even father said that mother was irresponsible. She left, after all. Who to trust? She ran the comb through her hair and it hurt. She looked at herself. She would trust her father this time. She grabbed a hair tie and wrapped her ratted hair up into a bundle. She did look pretty. A little bit.

I'll put on the dress and see how I feel, Patricia thought.

"Always follow your gut," that voice came back. Patricia dismissed it again. Father wouldn't hurt her, would he? Pleasure. Maybe she doesn't know anything. Maybe she needs to trust, something her mother couldn't do. God, she hated her mother right now for leaving her in this mess.

Music began to play downstairs. Sacred shit. She liked that word. Shit. Her mother started using it a lot toward the end of her parents' divorce.

Finally, dressed in white, like bride or maiden or whatever shit they call these dresses, Patricia left her room. Artwork was still on the walls. Childhood art of kites, ladybugs and birds her mother had painted.

She came to the living room filled with people, all grown ups. Many she didn't know but they were part of this community her Father liked. Women in frilly long dresses. Men looking weird. Everyone watched her as she came down the stairs. She felt naked even though she wore the dress. Like people saw her naked. The people were smiling like those crescent moons, like Asura. Their eyes sparkled like stars. It didn't feel right. But still, she didn't run.

"Beautiful" Father said. Asura stood next to him in her blue long dress, the one she had bought with Father on an island trip. Her hands were together in prayer.

Father was glowing, too. His eyes twinkled like the others. She liked it when father smiled at her but there went her tummy again. That funny feeling.

"Come, Patricia," Asura said.

Asura stood up. She was dressed elegantly. All white. All the women were in white. Men with long hair were chanting words she didn't understand.

Father stood up to welcome her to the circle.

"Friends. Here is my daughter. My blessed daughter."

Asura approached her. "Sit down, Patricia. Let me help you."

Patricia didn't like that, but she did it anyway. The funny feeling got worse.

"Here are beads for your divine experience. Rub them through your fingers and think about pleasure only. It's okay. Your father will be with you. It's a sacred dance between the father and you, the daughter. It's a dance for those of the highest state of consciousness, Patricia. An ancient dance. You're blessed. My own father did it for me. Many times. I loved my father, too. You see, this unites you and me forever on a level you'll appreciate one day. Like goddesses. You give your father great power for doing this. You would like to do that, wouldn't you?"

Patricia wanted to cry, but she held back.

saw her hesitation and then smiled. The black crescent moon, Patricia thought. That's what she'd call her forever, the Witch.

Asura put her finger to Patricia's lips. "But this is our secret. You're part of a secret world that is the most divine. You will penetrate the secrets of heaven tonight. Fly like an angel!"

Patricia closed her fists and felt the pain of her nails going into her hand. That pain she focused on and wouldn't let go. She thought of her 13th birthday in just one week. Birthday hats and doll cakes. She felt dirty. But surely Father would take care of her, wouldn't he? He would do what's right, wouldn't he?

The chanting began. The sound resonated through the room. In Patricia's bones. It was nice but it didn't feel right. Why?

Asura brought father to Patricia. "Patricia stand up for your blessed father". The chanting got louder. "Let your dress fall like a petal and show your flower, Patricia. Be proud of your sacred flower."

Patricia started to cry.

"Do you see, dear one, just like dew drops." tAsura urned to Patricia. "It's okay, honey. Let them flow. It's part of releasing. Part of cleansing. You see love is everything. Joy, sadness, pain and pleasure."

Asuralooked at Father and studied him. He hesitated. The chanting got louder.

A man stood up in the circle. He pushed his long grey hair away from his shoulders. Patricia remembered meeting him once before. On Christmas Day one month before.

"Charles, you are a great man. Show your daughter the beauty and the pain." You are her father. Her

blessed father. You'll rise to greatness on a new level of consciousness."

Charles closed his eyes and joined the chanting. Patricia began to cry harder.

"Lay down Patricia. We have butterflies and petals surrounding you. We are all together here for you."

Asura brought Father close to Patricia. "Breathe, feel love. It's all pure love." A beautiful daughter. She lifted Patricia's legs open. "It's a beautiful flower you have that will open like a spring day. That is why you are crying, Patricia. It's like a dewey spring day."

Patricia cried harder and as she did the chanting got even louder.

"Come Charles", said. God, she was beautiful. Divine. Perfect in every way. She had shown him the universe. His path.

Father knelt down remembering Patricia when she was a baby, holding her in his arms for the first time. Changing her diapers. Here she was now a near woman. Yes, this was the way. It makes perfect sense. A loving community surrounding him during this intimate, beautiful act. His community. One that he discovered. Not his wife.

He laid on top of Patricia..

Patricia cried out in pain, gripping the carpet. She left her body and went into her mind. Deep into her mind and became part of another world. It was her escape. Then she stopped crying. There was blood. There was blood everywhere. Others came close to her and touched her. Then they touched the blood and made a mark on their forehead. Patricia was numb. And looked at the both of them. "Now, we are family. Our secret."

Patricia looked upstairs and saw little Jimmy's eyes looking down through a door crack. His eyes were wide with fear. And he disappeared from that day forward. Father said he had died.

Patricia walked toward the figure in the corner and screamed. "You bitch. You witch!" And the woman spat at Patricia.

Mother grabbed Patricia. "Stop! Calm down!"

"What? You defend this witch? Do you know what she did to me? You raped me using my own father!" Patricia kicked the figure and spat again.

Mother grabbed Patricia again and looked her in the eye. "It's your time to rise above it. She used your body but not your soul. Never give her your soul. You must let it go."

"You want me to forgive the witch! Never!"

"Tonight you will feed her. You must pass through the hate. You mustn't hate at all. No hate in your heart. You must." Mother said.

"You want ME to feed this bitch! Are you out of your mind!" Patricia screamed.

"Trust me, Patricia. It's your soul that needs to be saved. Not hers. We've taken care of Asura."

Patricia couldn't believe her mother. Her mother was out of her mind, feeding and caring for a person such as this witch, one who stole her father away and then raped her own daughter? She couldn't even think of the right words to say. She ran. Patricia ran through the dark corridors, as the flowers from her hair fell. She sought the chamber where she first found herself in this seemingly underground world of hell, filth and evil lurking past. She curled tightly into her grandmother's quilt and cried alone.

The mother looked at . "Tonight we will feed you, dear Asura, with Patricia's help."

"No! screamed again. "I hate you all! Go to hell!"

Chapter Six

They were the guts, the entrails. The area people didn't like to go. Or didn't know existed. You had to enter from the back, where it was dark.

She liked it here though. The smell of algae growing on tubes. Festering. The dripping of pipes containing water that scientists labored over for Ph values, acidity, salinity and bacteria counts. This was their world. This is what brought life to Nature's World. Fake sea water to keep fish, Harry The Octopus and the penguins alive. Sometimes she'd watch the clustered starfish in the touch tank and wondered if they were really happy sitting on plexiglass, being stroked by two fingered children. There was no life in the water, no plankton like there was in the ocean. It was just the basic needs to keep them alive, like bread and water, she thought. But she couldn't tell anyone these ideas. These were bad ideas. Ungrateful, her father would say. Her father who loved this place. After all, he rescued all the animals from sure death, as he did the world. Why can't she be happy on the outside looking at all the beautiful fish swimming with iridescence colors, clown like lips and tales like angels? There was a truth behind the wall, where she was now sitting, and she felt tied to to it. She felt more comfortable here.

Sometimes she could feel the animals but she wouldn't tell anyone. She could read their thoughts. Then again maybe she was becoming like Jonathon, one of the crazy ones. Those who society is reluctant to trust. Those who are sent away to be reminded of a life that could have been. Destruction. War. Hate.

"You should be grateful," her father's words bubbled up inside her just like the gasses in the methane tank.

But, she trusted Jonathon. Even if some said he was dangerous and had the tattooed hand to prove it, she would meet with him by the dripping pipes, in the dark where the sea stars would take respite after a full day of exhibiting for crowds. They could talk about things. Everything. The way penguins walk. The dung beetles's nests and the sex club he'd been to the night before. And especially his friend Sam who would fuck him for only $20, a good rate. He felt like that was one good thing in his life.

Sometimes he'd grow angry that people are living in fear. And, he tell her that. He'd criticize her Father's world. She would hush him and look around. There weren't areas where someone else could hear you. But the ideas Jonathan told her were new thoughts for her. He told her that once people didn't pay for sex. Old people weren't sent away. Crazy people were the brilliant ones. In the old days the two of them could get it on without hygienic tests and monitoring. He didn't like how everything was controlled. He wished it could be free and open like they say society once was, or how they think it once was. The fact was, nobody knew since all the literature was lost during The Great Collapse.

Patricia knew how to calm him though. She had that force within her, just like when she walked the cougar by leash. Only with her was the cougar obedient and everyone marveled at her while walking it. When Jonathan got aggravated, she'd rest her hand on his shoulder to reassure him that she understood even when she didn't. She cared for him like a little brother. Sometimes she wondered if she loved him. That feeling in the stomach would rise. But, what was love, a manifestation of old literature and Disney characters. Love was not useful in society. She could fuck him, like she gets fucked at the centers. Sex, the simple human need that used to cause so much conflict. Monogamy, polygamy, judgments, diseases, unwanted births. When, in reality, humans are just animals designed to procreate. All the rest are what father calls stories crafted from the old Disney movies or what some people called literature.

When she was a teenager she'd find the salt mounds in the back chamber behind the generators. Like sand granules, she'd let the granules flow through her hands, like an hour glass. She'd taste the salt until her tongue shriveled. She'd feel herself too, become wet, wondering what a sex club would be like when she turned 18 and was allowed to go. She'd be tested like the waters for Ph values, acidity, salinity and bacteria counts. They'd read her pulse and create a chart so they could track her sexual interests, hygiene, reproductive cycles and partners. Imagine how people existed without these controls. She's feel the salt under her and she laid down, sometimes removing her clothes, feeling the rawness, like white sand, underneath her, remembering the beach days under the sun when she little. Those far off memories that seem like obscure dreams now. The humming of machines supplanted the sound of wind.

The corridors dripped from wetness and the halls extended to the feeding chambers where food was chopped, minced, pureed and mixed for perfection, to keep the animals alive and healthy. The smell made Patricia's stomach turn and she'd cover her mouth and nose.

When she was younger she'd sit and watch for hours the Amazon Room where fish would swim above her and she'd think what it'd be like to dive into water with piranha nibbling at her flesh. Her flesh. She feel her think about men nibbling at her too. She wondered how much that would cost. It's not penetration. Nor is it defined as alternative. She should be able to get a discount, she thought. She'd look around and wonder if others could hear her thoughts. Jonathan always could, it seemed. He'd see her thinking those thoughts and he'd laugh. But he wasn't there.

Patricia breathed into her oxygen mask. The herbal scent was nice. Pure oxygen. Good for the skin. Good for the heart. Dressed in long spiked black boots, she walked the street feeling good, thinking about that night when she'd hit the sex club. Her tests were all still positive, even her DNA was valued. She'd have to decide this year whether to donate her ovaries to the society, if she wanted, and contribute to the next pure generation. A privilege and an honor. Pure. And, she was reminded of her status with a stamp on the hand.

She entered Nature's World, the glass doors opened for her as they always do. But the levity stopped with the sound of crashing and screaming inside. She stopped.

"What's happening?" she asked the attendant in blue.

"He's gone mad. Jonathon,"

"Oh, no." Patricia ran toward the crashing. It can't be Jonathon.

Her spiked boots clicked loudly on the floor like an old forgotten morse code operator. She remembered the lesson, of contrivance. SOS, the signal came to her. Why was she thinking these absurd thoughts? Jonathon. Then she saw father standing there with the guards. His cane was erect, like a spear next to him. Jonathon.

He was going mad. Glass was everywhere. On the floor. A large jagged piece, like a dagger, was in his hands and he was swinging at the guards. Penguins were fluttering about and water swished out of the pool. Animals throughout the Center were screaming and crying, it seemed. Even the fish. The fish? Why was her mind doing this to her?

She got close the fray and was yanked by the guard. "Get away, Patricia." Were those her father's words or the guard's?

"Leave him alone." She yanked her arm away.

"Jonathon. What's wrong? Tell me. What happened. Talk to me!"

Jonathon looked at her and for a moment his wild, frightened eyes, settled into a softness like that of a deer. She could hear his thoughts. Something was wrong.

"He's gone absolutely mad. We cannot have these kind of people working here. How do we screen for this?"

That was her father talking. She could hear him despite the loud sounds. Last year Betsy had gone mad like Jonathon. She had tried to smuggle frogs out of the center. One was in her mouth. She was caught. The year before that someone had tried to sabotage the salinity tanks. They said they were on the fish's side. Crazy people, father had said.

"Jonathon!"

It cost $100 now. It was the one good thing in my life, Patricia."

"My god." Maybe he was nuts. But, what is "crazy"? "Jonathon, is it only that?"

"The penguins always tell me how unhappy they are. They want to be free. Why does it all cost so much for everyone, Patricia. Why can't we be free?"

He dropped the shard of glass and the guards jumped on him. He was no longer resisting. He was sobbing uncontrollably like a child. The penguins walked on the glass creating streaks of bloody paths. She saw that Jonathan's hands were bleeding too.

"I'll get you out, Jonathon. I promise," she said as he was dragged away.

Father approached Patricia, placing his hand on her shoulder.

"Patricia."

She didn't respond. She was still looking at the blood.

"He is unstable. You have to leave him alone. He'll be taken care of."

"Where?"

"The same place we are taking care of the others. We are trying to understand mental illness, Patricia. This is a concern we all have. You must understand that."

"He said he could hear the animals, Father. He could hear their thoughts."

"That's exactly why he needs help, Patricia." He scanned the room.

"Look, do you see the snakes there?" He pointed to another glass cage. "Can you hear what they are saying?"

She stopped. She wanted to tell him that she too has feelings about the starfish, about the giant sea bass and the angel fish. Special feelings, like the ability to hear them. "No, I can't hear the snakes, Father." He frightened her.

"Neither can I. Neither can they." and he lifted his cane and used it to scan the room of all the others watching.

"Tell me, who is the crazy one making up these stories and creating so much danger around us?"

She couldn't speak.

"Say it. Jonathon."

"I can't say it. What if he is special?"

"As I said, he is going to a special place."

Father. You had said in your meeting that that special place is being filled with too many special people. The crazies. People are talking about it, you know.

"What are they saying."

"There's not enough room in those special places anymore." Patricia said.

"It's time you come a meeting, Patricia. Maybe it's time you grow up. It's time for you to learn leadership and making difficult decisions," Father said.

Chapter Seven

～ ～

"Wake up, sleepy head. Wake up."

Patricia woke up looking at doll's head with a dangling tooth. Behind that head was another one, that of a wild looking child with ratted hair and flowers. "It's time to grow up!"

This jarred Patricia. Had she been merely dreaming? Or was she remembering? Her thoughts were so wrapped up in feelings that she couldn't make sense of anything. The dropped out of the doll's mouth, making Lily giggle.

Lily jumped up next to Patricia. "Mother has something planned for you. Only the big kids get to do it. Those who are ready to meet the devil."

"What are you talking about, Lily?"

"The devil that is inside of us all. We have to get rid of it. Mother likes to call it an exorcism!" Lily laughed.

"But, Mother tells me I don't have a devil in me. I'm pure angel! Even my toots sound like an angel singing, Mother says!" Lily smiled and then put the tooth in her mouth and smiled at Patricia.

"You are all crazy. And I thought people in my father's world were crazy."

"Oh, that world. The Overworld. Here we are human. There they are monsters."

Patricia grew quiet. And then there was a distant sound of a gong.

"Oh, goody. We get to cook you up now!"

"Cook ME?"

"Oh, no, you get to do the cooking and feed the monster tonight!" Lily stopped."Oops, I shouldn't have said that. Don't tell Mother, please."

Patricia was having memories of her father's girlfriend and the night she was raped. "What are you talking about?"

"Oh, don't worry, Patricia. We're all about love here!"

Patricia had her guard up, prepared to flee. She knew the escape route now. But where would she go? There was no where to go.

She walked slowly and carefully to the kitchen, following Lily who lead her. They entered a dark room with cauldrons over fires. Along the walls there were shelves with a line up of jars filled with herbs. Pots and pans hung on the ceiling. It smelled moist like mushrooms.

"Here she is Mother!" Lily called out.

And, indeed, there was Mother with a big smile on her face. "Oh, my dear. It's a special night for you! We will be cleansing your soul tonight. Are you ready?"

"What the fuck are you talking about?"

"Oh, honey, please don't use such dirty, foul language around here. Better to use clean language."

Patricia noticed a irony in that statement.

"Please, Lily, introduce Patricia to the fungus cabinet and take out the Boletes, chanterrelles, hedgehogs and witches butter and then we can start cooking the meal."

"Witches butter?"

The mother continued to stir a large cauldron of soup. Others in the kitchen were chopping something big. What was it?

"This is my favorite room in the world, Patricia. Most of all these collections are MINE! Welcome to the world beyond Willie Wonka! That what Mother says but I don't know what a willie is. But I figured out what a wonk is, do you want to hear it?"

No, I don't!

They entered a vast room where glass jars sat filled with dried mushrooms, herbs, barks, roots and flowers. Patricia had never seen such a vast supply of such food. And then she saw another shelf filled with foods she hadn't seen for years, maybe decades. Cereal boxes of Lucky Charms, Fruit Loops, Pop Tarts and Twinkies. "Oh, my god! How old is this food and where did you get it?"

"Oh, those are the special treats used only used once a year. For birthday celebrations. The food lives forever, did you know that?. Loopy always demands a bowl of Fruit Loops for his birthday. That's why we call him Loopy." Lily giggled. Lily continued walking deeper into the room. "Here are all our medicines. We have everything. See? We are very sophisticated."

Patricia marveled at all they had squirreled away. Some of the herbs she recognized, being reminded of her childhood when her parents wildcrafted with her in the fields and in the forests. They were the happiest days. So long ago.

There were a set of fanciful containers made of porcelain. Patricia opened the top to see what looked like soil or something else?

"What are these for, Lily?"

"Oh, don't touch those! That's Uncle Joe and Aunt Susan. They died last year. We haven't gotten around to scattering them yet."

Patricia set the lid down quickly. "Those are ashes? Dead people?"

"Yeah. Don't you have dead people in the Overworld? We have lots of dead people! They are the most fun!"

"What do you mean, Lily?"

"Dead people, the spirits. They are with us every day! In fact, Uncle Joey is standing right behind you."

Patricia turned around while a cold chill rushed through her. This child scared her at times. Mother called.

"Patricia! Come stir this pot. It's almost ready for tasting!"

She couldn't deny it. Like Willy Wonka's world, everything around her seemed fascinating, dangerous, enthralling. She did help her mother stir the pot and Patricia couldn't tell what was in the pot. But it did smell good and she was getting hungry.

"We eat in one hour! Lily dear, maybe you can help get dear Patricia get ready."

"Ready for what?" Patricia asked.

"Tonight you must purge all hatred and anger, so you're free. Completely free. We will have a celebration in your honor. Because it's time for you to rise to a new level."

These words mother was speaking sounded horrific and again she was reminded of that night of her rape. Would her own mother do something as horrific? Her own father had. Who can Patricia trust? Her head was spinning.

"Come, Patricia. I'll brush your hair and put new flowers in your hair."

Patricia went along with it. But she was on guard. She would kick and scream this time, if anyone touched her, even if such an act risked her life. She will never succumb to that same power of domination again. Ever.

The time had come. Another gong was heard down the halls. Patricia's hair was brushed gently by Lily. And they walked together to the Great Den. And it was upon entering the den that Patricia had to control a scream that was rising from her belly.

There sitting in the middle upon an elegant chair was the witch. The people sat around her waiting and the witch, Asura, started to cry and scream. "Fuck you, all!"

Mother walked in holding a large bowl with a spoon. "Patricia, join me. We are going to feed these woman. We are giving her the best of what we have before we even begin to eat ourselves. This poor woman has not eaten all day. Poor Asura," Mother shook her head.

"I hate you! I hate you all!" Asura screamed out.

"What, you're not hungry dear? You haven't eaten for days, always denying the best, which is what you always sought, my dear. And here we give it to you. We prepare it for you. I After all the work we have done for you? My, my, my," Mother said and sat next to her.

"Now, you're not going to upset the food bowl again. Are you?" Mother said to Asura. "Okay, now open wide?"

Asura grimaced and looked away at first and then opened her mouth for the food as Mother spooned it. "That's a good Asura. I have lots of food for you!" Everyone watched and sat quietly, staring at Asura with a smile.

"Why are you feeding her?" Patricia burst out. "She's a horrible person! Why give her anything after what she did to you and to me!"

"Because I am NOT her, Patricia. I have no hate in my heart, but plenty of sympathy. I will never allow her hate and evil enter my heart or my soul. I choose NEVER to give her that power over me." Mother turned to Asura, "Open wide. It's the best food we have! All for you before we even feed ourselves. That's how generous and compassionate we are here, Asura."

Patricia couldn't believe it. She couldn't believe what she was watching.

"Come, Patricia. It's your turn to feed her. And never let her hate feed you."

Everyone watched Patricia. Where could Patricia run? There was no where to go. So, she stepped forward next to Asura and took the spoon. She wanted to whack Asura with it. Plunge the spoon into her eyes. Make her choke on it. All these ideas and more spun into her mind as she held the spoon in front of Asura's mouth. Asura would not look at Patricia and Asura's face was contorted, her teeth showing. Patricia looked at her more closely, at the deep wrinkles that had grown on her face. Her hair which was once so flowing was ragged and knotted. Even her eyes looked different, not young, but like someone filled with rage.

"Feed her, Patricia. And let it all go," her mother said, standing stoically by her side.

Patricia raised the spoon to Asura's lips and like rapid dog, Asura took the food into her mouth and spat it at Patricia. "I hate you."

"Don't let her hate bother you," Patricia. Mother said. "Be stronger. She's like a child. Treat her as such. With pure love," Mother said wiping Asura's face with a towel and handing it to Patricia.

"I hate you all!" Asura said.

"Now, should we put you back in your room so you can think about what you just did or are you going to eat your meal, Asura dear?" Mother said.

Patricia began to understand. She understood the game. "Yes, Asura. I have your food. Eat and enjoy." Patricia smiled and then looked at mother. The two now understood one another. Patricia almost started to laugh. She arrived. She knew to release the hate and to smile. "Another spoonful, Asura. Shall we try again?"

Mother looked at Patricia with a smile. "I always knew how smart you were. Never let their evil become your own . . . always be kind. Always."

Patricia never felt such emotions before. Letting go. The weight of the world off her shoulders. The feeling all these years of hatred. Gone. Just like that. With such simple acts.

"You know Asura was abused as a child by her own father. She continued the cycle. We are stopping it."

Asura began to cry.

"Jimmy, it's time for Asura to leave and for the rest of us to enjoy our supper."

The two of them left and more food was brought into what seemed like a full celebration of laughter and joy amongst the people. A feeling Patricia hadn't had or seen in so long. Lily even got up to dance and people laughed. Patricia even laughed for the first time in years. And it scared her a little. Once you feel good it makes the ugly disappear.

Patricia looked up to see Loopy. His teeth were black again and he smiled. He walked over to her.

"I stole a bowl of Fruit Loops. Do you want to come join me?" Loopy asked, like a flirt.

She didn't like the way he was looking at her. She was in a hell hole six feet underground. Where in life was a place where hell did not exist? She wondered.

The colony prepared for sleep in the Big Den again. Patricia now knew the rhythm, just after two days. Is that how much time she had been there? It seemed like years. Lily came to her as the lights dimmed. "Tonight we go again. But this time we go all the way."

Patricia was tired of figuring out riddles. And so she closed her eyes until hours later she again felt that clawing on her shoulder.

"It's time to go!" Lily whispered.

She saw Jimmy's shadow waiting.

They climbed again the Great Tower, like a cathedral, the inside of a hallow redwood tree. They flew again across the forest on vines through a moonlit night. Patricia knew what to do when Lily or Jimmy told her to duck under the ferns. A drone would surely come close and then disappear into the darkness. Were the trees really talking? Patricia grew weary of the guesses, but she soaked in the moonlight. The moon was full and she could feel the light on her in a way she had never experienced before.

Together they walked along a creek. Tip toeing on rocks. The water was cold and soon Patricia's feet felt numb and she liked it, remembering day in her childhood walking barefoot all summer. The light shimmered in the water and Patricia kept noticing the droplets turning into bigger concentric waves.

Then she began to hear it and fear began to grow. She stopped dead remembering that smell, one she had not inhaled in thirty years or more.

"Get your mask on fast," Father had said. The news had gone crazy. It was the end of times, so everyone screamed. The fear was tremendous. It had just been the day before visiting the beach with her Father when they witnessed all the dead sea life on the beach - birds, fish and every other critter one could imagine. The sea had turned toxic. And it was within days the toxicity grew into the air, killing coastal residents, Islanders and more.

She had a mask. Her father had kept it for her and it was only for the chosen ones, the ones who knew the truth. Her father had even rescued animals and more. Those who survived deemed him a hero.

The death was something extraordinary. Not a single war in the history of the world took so many lives within weeks.

Patricia had forgotten. She had forgotten all of this. And it came washing over her. The guilt. The fear. The relief.

"They deserved it, Patricia," he had said to her. They were stupid and they were ignorant, not doing anything about climate change or the world's problems. They wanted something called freedom. Freedom to exploit and freedom to chase greed, never understanding that their actions had consequences.

Maybe her father was right. But that one night as they watched the people die on screen, the drones circled through the community, she saw her Father smile.

"Serves them right," he had said.
And she shuddered.

"It's the ocean. It's poisonous." Patricia stood in fear.

Jimmy and Lily looked at Patricia. No, it's okay. It's okay!

"You hear it, don't you?"

"It will kill us! The poison. The toxicity," Patricia said.

"No, that's not true, Patricia. It was lie," Jimmy said.

"A lie? What do you mean?"

"Yes, the water was very unhealthy, but that wasn't what killed the people. That was a lie. They killed the people. The released a virus that killed them to make it look like it was the ocean. To make it look like the end of The Book."

"Father killed the people?"

Jimmy looked away.

"Father said he saved life. He saved the planet."

"Maybe he did. What do I know. But I do know the ocean is there. Let's go"

"What are you talking about Jimmy?"

And then there it was, just off in the distance. A body she had not seen in years. One she had to forget. That beauty. The ocean.

"You go, Jimmy and Patricia. I'll keep watch. If you hear the whistle. You have to hide!"

Jimmy grabbed Patricia's hand and like two children, as they had been together years ago, they ran across the sandy beach under the starry night right into the surf. A biolumence began to shine and vibrate under the vast stars. They were alone in the world. Surely it felt that way.

The cool water immediately splashed memories into Patricia's mind, those she had forgotten. That feeling of sand between toes. That rush of energy with every wave. The tumbling shells covering the beach. Even in her youth there had never been so much life around her. The water glistened with the stars above. A dolphin jumped out of the water in the moonlight. She had never felt so alive.

"People take from Nature, Patricia. That's why we cut The Wild Lands off to stupid people." she heard her father. But she decided to drown him out. The water, the beach, the stars . . . they were exquisite! And even her brother laughed.

"It's beautiful!" she screamed. She didn't want the moment to end but it ended fast and dangerously.

The loud whistle could have been a bird, but Jimmy knew better.

"Get down, low, close to the water and don't say a word."

They laid down flat on the surf next to the large rocks. The drones were coming. Many of them this time. Twenty or maybe thirty? That was odd and Patricia knew it. They were looking for something or someone. And she shuddered to think that it might be her. Should she jump up and claim innocence? Could she turn in her own brother and her own mother and these crazy filthy people who lived like insects?

"She looked at her brother. His eyes were wide, watching. He looked at her. "Close your eyes and look down. Their scanning devices look for eyes and we're already at risk with heat energy. Pray."

Just then a flock of bird flew from the trees. Hundreds of them. Or could they have been thousands. Jimmy let out a howl. "Look who came to save us!"

The birds confused the drones and they flew away.

Lily came running down the beach. "They got 'em, didn't they Jimmy!"

Patricia and Jimmy pulled themselves out to the water, dripping wet with sand and salt water.

"Look!"

Patricia pointed to the trees. A large eagle, white and glistening under the moonlight, stood on top of a tall redwood tree. It looked like a star with its wing extended wide. And it called loudly.

Lily gasped. "Patricia, it's called to you. Oh, you are so lucky. It came for you!"

"What are you saying, Lily?"

"The eagle is your totem animal! You are being called, as a visionary. To see what needs to be seen and to fly!"

She giggled and Jimmy spoke.

"An eagle flies higher than any other bird. It's the messenger from the spirit world. And it's come to tell you about freedom and the courage to look ahead. For some reason, it believes you are honest."

"Jesus, that's a lot of weight you're putting on me for just seeing a bird."

"No, Patricia," Lily said. "The eagle sought you. It's telling you that you now must follow your path, your destiny. It's time." Lily burst out with a giggle. "Time to hurry back, Jimmy. The sun will rise soon!"

As they ran back to the colony, they harvested soap root, blackberries, laurel leaves and even mugwart. Then rain began to fall. And thunder clapped. A storm was coming. She was almost feeling like a child again. Feeling everything. Feeling free and wild.

Chapter Eight

~ ~

When they returned to the colony everyone was awake and they were packing up rapidly.

"What's going on?" Jimmy asked.

"We're not safe here. We need to move. During the night the drones hovered for an inordinate amount of time," Loopy said.

"We saw them, too," Lily said.

"They are coming. We can feel it. But a storm is coming, too, and it can be our cover if we act fast. Thank you to nature."

Several spiders crawled past Jimmy and smashed them with his foot.

Patricia watched him do it without apologizing.

"The wind is beginning. Time to move. Two hours!" a voice echoed down the dark dirty halls.

Jimmy sat in the room alone with Patricia. She sat cross legged on the bed wrapped in her hair blanket. She was so tired. She just needed to stare into the darkness.

"I'm worried about you." Mother had said to her the night before. "Watch her, Jimmy."

The LEDs gave them some light in the dusty room. She could see the whites of Jimmy's eyes and see the stubble on his thick cheeks and some on his fingers. She watched him whittle a stick with a knife with sharp teeth. She wasn't sure whether to be afraid or feel safe by his action. For the moment, she was just numb. She couldn't feel anything. She missed home, the comfort. The sex. All of it. Each moment she sat in this underground tomb, she could feel herself become more lost, even if she had found her long lost mother.

"Do you dance in your world? In Father's world?"

"Dance? We have a loving society, Jimmy. Clean. Safe. You guys live like insects."

"We have lots of love." He smiled, then licked the knife again.

"Love? Oh, that thing. There's no such thing, Jimmy."

He cocked his head. Holding the knife, she felt that fear again.

"Love is a manipulation of the senses. There's no such thing. Attraction? Yes. Love, no."

"You've never made love before?" Jimmy sat up straight.

She paused. She grew more afraid, but what did she have to lose? Surely her brother wouldn't rape her.

"It's called sex. Fucking. We have evolved."

"Fucking." he said it as a statement, like he was tasting the word.

"Fucking. Yes. People fuck just like animals. It's biology. It's not love," Patricia said like he should know. Still she covered the hair blanket around her body, feeling more secure with it for the first time.

Jimmy didn't move. He continued to swish the word around his mind. Then he put the knife away in its case.

"Is that what you guys do?"

"Isn't that what you do you here?"

"No." Jimmy said. He looked disgusted.

"Of course you guys fuck. He have kids here. Society would disappear without people fucking."

"People fucking. When people fall in love they make love."

"For the first time, Patricia started to laugh. She fell back on her bed and burst into hysterics. You guys really do live like the stone age! Tell me, you guys aren't monogamous still, are you?"

Jimmy didn't like her laughing at him. The whites of his eyes grew wider. And his brows furled. He looked a little embarrest, too.

She looked at him more. "My god. Bound feet and monogamy are one in the same. Cutting off pleasure and what nature gave you. You guys revel in the world of nature, but you can't face what you really are." For the first time, she looked more curious about this world. Engaged.

"What do you guys do?" Jimmy asked. He looked more relaxed now and curious, as well.

"Well, when we need sex, just like any animal, we go to a sex bar."

"What's a sex bar?"

"It's a place to have sex and pay for it. It used to all be for free and spread disease. Now we can control these natural societal urges and it even helps the economy."

"You have to pay for it? That's prostitution."

"No!" she laughed again.

"It used to be called prostitution, but they were the honest ones. Prostitutes understood the true nature of humans. Yet, they were persecuted. Just like the homosexuals once. Just like women who had babies out of wedlock. Oh, tell me, do people still get married in your world?"

"You're a slut then," Jimmy said and he spat on the ground.

"Yes! Thank you. I have fucked over 1326 men and women. It's pretty average. But, sex can get expensive." She hadn't seen him spit.

His mouth dropped. Then she understood his reaction.

"You think that is weird, don't you." Patricia said.

"It's disgusting."

"I'll tell you what's disgusting," Patricia paused, as if trying to collect her thoughts. "Throughout history people have placed value on sex as if it's a bad thing unless it's done as society says it should. It made no sense. Diseases bred, there were unwanted pregnancies, there was hurt and rape. It tore societies apart. Everyone lived under a veneer of riotousness and not truth. We are a truthful society, Jimmy. Everyone is safe. Love is a veneer too. You can care for people, many people. But sex has nothing to do with any of it." Patricia stared at Jimmy and for the first time she noticed that she was scaring him a bit now.

"Love? Love? I mean, just look at what love did for Mom and Dad!"

Jimmy looked away and stood up. "We have to get ready to move"

One by one they exited the underground dwelling and climbed the great Redwood Tower. They swung by branches helping one another and then hid in the fern grove until they were gathered and ready to go. The rain had started and the thunder was clapping. Then carefully they began a journey through the woods until they reached an outcropping of rocks which they climbed high, leading to a single track trail on the edge of a precipice. The wind began to whip and they were silent as they walked, holding carefully to the few possessions they had. Some boxes of food, blankets and water.

The wind kicked up and Patricia was getting tired. The journey was getting more arduous as the earth became more wet and slippery. And that's when it happened. She started to slip and then grabbed what was behind it her. It was Asura behind her and that made Asura slip even more.

"Help!" Asura was falling, holding on to a singular branch as her body fell over the cliff. Patricia was there holding her other hand.

"Help me sister," Asura said. Her eyes wide, blue glistening that turned into a sparks of fear.

Patricia held it when a wave of emotions set upon, looking straight into the eyes of a person who had brought her such great hate for so many years.

"I am not your sister. Call me who I am." She screamed with rage. Her arms trembled and she held Asura's hand tightly, working to bring her up. But she was slipping too.

"Sister. We are sisters. Remember."

"Call me what I am!" Their eyes locked. The wind kept blowing, as rain plummeted down. The earth started to give way under Patricia and she was getting pulled down too.

Asura looked down and then back to Patricia. "You are the child I raped because I wanted love for myself so bad. I'm so sorry." And with those words, Asura released her grip of Patricia.

"Oh, my god! Patricia screamed. And she watched Asura fall onto the granite rocks below,."

"No!" Patricia cried out.

Mother came to Patricia. "You released her."

"No! She let go! I didn't release her. I didn't kill her!" Patricia said defensively screaming as rain and mud covered her.

"You released her on the highest level possible. You freed her. What you did will last her for eternity. She is free now forever, at least of what she created in this life."

"What?" Patricia looked at her mother.

"You saved her, Patricia. You saved her soul. I'm not sure I wouldn't been so kind," Mother said. "Now, you are free too." And she hugged Patricia.

"Why is it all so hard? I want to go back to Father's world where I could be happy."

"It's just a veneer, Patricia. A pure illusion, full of lies. It will all crumble soon. You'll see. There is always enlightenment after the darkness. And this darkness is darker than anything I could ever imagine. Then, I will believe the light will be glorious. Just wait. You'll see."

After hours of walking through the storm they arrived at a cave and entered. Inside the cave they had to swim threw a small river until they reached a dark cavern filled with candles along the wall. A cathedral with stalagtites and stalagmites glistening like jewels, Lily shouted out "I'm going treasure hunting tomorrow!" Otherwise, there was complete silence except for the drips that echoed through the cave.

"It's time to rest now. We're safe, for now." Mother said. "Tomorrow we have a celebration."

"We just ran for our lives. Somebody died and you want a party?" Patricia asked her mother.

"Oh, sweetheart. That was small potatoes compared to how we've been living."

Patricia didn't ask more. She didn't want to learn more. It was time to rest and she was wet and exhausted.

It was in no time, though, Patricia woke up to see her brother leave the room. She decided to follow him. Where was he going? She was careful with her steps, following his distant shadow through the dark cave. More corridors. And then he disappeared. She stopped. Where did he go? Then she saw it. A room behind a large stone. Just a crack of line with light was coming from the other side and she peered in between the crack, leaning against the stone. And then it fell and she fell on top of it with a crash.

Jimmy looked at her in shock. But she wasn't looking at him. She was looking behind him to a vast wall and she couldn't believe her eyes.

"You bitch. Why did you follow me?"

"Oh, my God," Patricia said with complete awe. She stood up, not even paying attention to aches of her legs. "Did you do this, Jimmy? Does Mother know?"

There was no use for Jimmy to hide it from Patricia. She saw it. She saw all of it. What he had done. What he had been doing. She had found him out. His secret. His secret for years. Acorn caps, turkey tail mushrooms. Wires and conduits. Even caps from Pepsi coke bottles. One might mistake the contraption for a mess unless you were able to understand computer systems. There was a screen, an old screen from years ago. And there was her father. He was walking down the hall at the Nature Center. "Did you build this and why am I seeing Father on the screen?"

"I monitor him. To stop him from monitoring us."

"What the fuck, brother? What do you mean?"

Jimmy sat down on his chair. An old chair that squeaked when he rocked. "Father sends insects here. He knows everything. They try to watch us. But I watch them more."

"So, those spiders you killed? Those were sent by Father?"

"Yep. And I send crickets to his Natural World. I call them 'Jimmy Crickets. I always liked Jimeny."

Patricia's jaw dropped. "And do your crickets talk?"

"They whisper, Patricia." Jimmy said. "The world is full of temptations. Let you conscience be your guide," Jimmy laughed.

Patricia needed to sit down. "I don't know if you're a sick human being, insane or brilliant. I don't know anything. I know nothing." Patricia paused, marveling at the system. "And what does Mother know about this?"

"She knows nothing and nothing you shall tell her. This is about Father and I. Not her and Father."

"Oh, my God. We are one fucked up family."

"All those years of video games paid off. When dad sends in a spider, I send in a cricket. I call them the Darwin Wars."

"And does Father know that you monitor him?"

"No."

Patricia had to marvel at the computer system. A work of art, a beast her brother had created with junk, pure junk. A tin can system. And she looked at him differently. She actually had respect for him.

"He does know you're here. That was why the drones flew looking for us. You have to return soon.

Back to The Island. You have to stop all of it. I'll have your back. And we have an army inside who have been listening to my crickets." Jimmy smiled with satisfaction. "They have a conscious now."

"And the talking trees? Are you behind that too?"

"No, not I." He smiled but it was hard to know that smile. What was behind that smile?

"So, we are creating world peace with spiders and talking crickets. You know, if there is ever peace in the world, I choose never to tell anyone this story. I knew we were a fucked family before. But now we set a whole new standard. We'll make any family in the world look good."

"We're special," Jimmy smiled.

"So, how am I supposed to stop everything? You know what he's trying to do, right?"

"Yes, kill the mentally ill and the elderly, as well as the Mushroom Colony."

Patricia stopped him. "No, he wants me to do the killing. He wants me to lead The Island."

"So, it's easy. Kill his computer system. Unlock the vaults with the so called mentally ill. And run like fucking hell. Lily releases the banana slugs on cue and we shut down FAN, inc. MOO will not know what to do and we'll have it in control."

"Right. Banana slugs wearing Superman capes? You couldn't make this shit up."

"I got you covered. And, yes, I did make the shit up."

"You know, the moment Father sees me he will likely kill me."

"Don't worry. I've got a cricket in place and ready for action."

"And your cricket does kung fu?"

Jimmy didn't reply.

"I'm sorry, Jimmy. I know you're trying. But you have no idea how evil Father has become. I'll try. But there is this thing. I don't know what to believe in anymore. Everything has been a lie in my life. Everything.

"Maybe you just have to believe in yourself," Jimmy said.

The words comforted Patricia. Her little brother was no longer so little. And right now he seemed bigger than her.

"I'm sorry, Jimmy. All those years I hated you. I based that judgment on you being a little boy. I'm really proud to have you as a brother."

"Oh, fuck you. Don't get all sissy on me. And you need to return to the others. Do not tell anyone about this. I'll be hanged."

"What do you mean?"

"We have a rule. No technology. And if you do, the colony has a right to hang you."

"Fuck. So Mother could hang you for this and she's been telling you that Father would put you in prison? You've been walking the razor's edge, brother. My lips are sealed. Promise.

Chapter Nine

～ ～

Sleeping in a cave. The drip drip. The echoes. The quiet. Patricia stirred, tightening her quilt around her, trying to feel secure and put together, holding it all together in the bare ground of rock. Does she dare open her eyes to break this feeling of a bit of comfort. She opens one eye. There in no one in the room. The room is empty except for the lit candles. She opens the other eye and sits up. Where has everyone gone?

She begins a walk, back tracking the way they had entered. She hears a murmuring from afar, as if coming from the outside of the cave. Had they been caught by her father? Maybe they had left her to protect themselves? So many questions began to spin her head and she found herself walking faster as the cave became darker.

Then, far away she saw the light. The light at the end of the cave. Outside. There were voices. So, she decided to go carefully with stealth and to find out what was going on.

There was a howling unlike anything she had ever heard. It frightened her again, but she was becoming accustomed to this feeling. She'd been in fear of her father, Jonathon's fate, her own escape, the wild child, her brother. Her mother.

Finally, she emerged from the cave into the forest. The wind was roaring loud. She saw Lily and Mother."Why are you out here?" she said as the blanket that wrapped around her flew off like a cape down the valley revealing her ragged shirt and underwear. Long hair smacked her face hard and she held it back to clear her eyes. But she didn't care about those things because she saw something that made her stop and watch.

People. They were dancing, writhing and pulsating with the wind. Pushing against it. Twisting with it. The high notes of flutes ripped into her, as if through her flesh and straight to her bones, as fierce as the wind twisting around her. Drummers beat drums wildly. There was chaos but yet rhythm too. She'd never heard music like this before with wind screaming. She'd never seen musicians let alone hear them. That feeling.

All the people pulsated to the rhythm as the branches of the trees seemed to follow, all together, as if the entire forest and colony were coalescing into a dance together. Possessed souls. All was alive. Then there was a crack and a redwood branch fell off a redwood tree landing right in front of Patricia. She gasped in fear and jumped away, feeling afraid, feeling the energy was too much for her. Nobody looked but Lily who pointed and giggled at Patricia. She came running out of the circle of dancers. The half naked child was pounding the ground with her two feet, turning, twisting like a possessed soul. Her long dirty hair was tied under her chin like an old man's beard. She rolled her stomach in waves and gave off a screeching sound like once Patricia had heard from a juvenile monkey who had been reunited with its mother at the Center. She had studied it. She was studying Lily.

"Patricia, you are joining us!" Lily pulled Patricia into the middle, she couldn't resist. "Do this Patricia. Do it!"

Patricia couldn't. She didn't know what to do. The energy pulsated through her like charges of electricity. She was frozen. Shocked.

But the bodies excited her. She watched the men move their muscles, dark skin, joints. Shoulders. Her body felt alive. Bewitched.

"The tree wanted to take your hand and dance! The limb. It was asking to dance with you." Lily giggled fiercely.

"Lily, the branch nearly killed me." Patricia said loud.

Lily laughed her wicked laugh. "NO! If it wanted to do that it would have landed on you. Trees are smart!"

Lily stopped smiling and got close to Patricia.

"And did it land on you?" She said this in a serious tone, defensively.

"No, it didn't"

"See? The spirits like you!"

"It scared the hell out of me."

"Hell?" She started to laugh "Consider, just consider, it wanted to awaken you to the universe. FEEL the fear. Accept it. Then you can be free, Patricia." Lily opened her eyes wide again. Her gaze stabbed Patricia. A truth killing a lie. But how could such silly things be true. "So silly." Lily said, like reading Patricia's thought. Then she laughed and ran off dancing into the crowd, yelping like a dog. It chilled Patricia. A wild child.

Patricia looked beyond to see Jimmy straddling his legs wide as Lily ran through them, the way Father used to play.

It started to rain suddenly and the crowd looked up to the sky laughing and clapping. Many started to remove their clothes. "Over here" one shouted. A bucket of blossoms were passed around and each grabbed a fistful spreading them over their bodies. The smell. It was sweet.

Mother came to Patricia. She was half naked too and it embarrassed Patricia to see a woman, her own mother, with sagging breasts and wrinkled skin and be so free with her body. She had never seen a body so ill taken care of. How easy surgery would be and body repaired. It almost sickened her. But it was her mother. She was beginning to accept this even if she didn't want to.

"Take some!" her mother said.

"What are they?"

"Blossoms and soap root. To wash. A shower from heaven!"

Patricia just stood there as the rain streaked through her hair and down her body. She started to cry. But nobody could tell. This was a different kind of crying than before. She could feel it. It was like the music, the air, the water was filling her spirit, making her recognize how hollow she had felt before then. She didn't want it though. She wanted to feel this was all wrong and yet it felt so good. Like she was getting away with something. And she wanted more. Patricia felt alive. And as she looked around she began to smile and feel grateful for feeling something she had never experienced before, knowing the feeling could stop in a heartbeat but the memory of this moment was now a part of her soul.

It was that very evening after the washing party Mother sat down with Patricia. "It's time to talk and time to plan. Tomorrow you return to Father."

Patricia was beginning to understand. But she had to face her most fierce opponent. Her own father.

Jimmy came to join them. And sat quietly. "Jimmy and Loopy have it worked out for you to sneak into the tunnels that are connected here to the cave. It'll take some time, but you can do it. Be ready for your father. And then be ready for us.

"Father will kill me," Patricia said.

"No, he won't. He'd prefer to see you suffer but you still are valuable to him. And remember something that can hold you together."

Patricia listened.

"This was never a test from the universe of who could save the earth. It was never a game of who had power or control. It was a test of who could love without hate. Who could lead with heart and not spite. That is the ultimate game in life. Never hate. Never give them that power because those who lead and who are not complete themselves will use you to complete themselves. Love and have compassion. Always. Find stillness. Never forget how to dance. And remember, life is but a journey."

"Mother, I think we're done with the lecture," Jimmy stopped Mother.

"I did go on too much. My apologies. There are so many things I wish I could have shared with you, my daughter, of these last thirty years. Though I lost that time with you, I have to remain grateful that you are alive and that you have a big journey ahead of you."

"What do you mean, Mother?"

"You are destined to take on the world. To be a leader."

"I don't want to be a fucking leader. You sound like Father now."

"You'll know when the time comes. And you have a brother who will stand at your guard. Right, Jimmy? Without jealousy. Without vanity. But with pure brotherly love."

Jimmy looked away and bit his lip. I can do more, Mother."

"Jimmy, you'll have to do what your heart guides you to do. That I cannot change."

Patricia looked at Mother. "Is that what Father wanted of you?"

"What do you mean, Patricia?"

Patricia stood up and turned around, feeling more confident than ever before. "Did dad want you to stand by him as you are asking Jimmy to stand by me? Is that what happened? Is that why Father is angry? If you talk about giving and loving, why didn't you stand with Father?"

A spider walked by Jimmy, and he smashed it with his fists.

There was silence. An awkward long moment of silence. The dripping of the water around them in the dark cave grew louder. The long echoes through the dark caverns that surrounded them were like calls from another time and place. And they could all feel it. There were no more words to say.

The look on Mother's face was one of horror. She striked Patricia across the face. And walked away.

Patricia looked at Jimmy, holding her cheek that burned. "Why am I always the one to get beat up?"

"You're the chosen one?" And he shrugged his shoulders and curved his lips into a smile.

"Fuck you," she said.

And with that her brother wrapped his arms around her and they hugged for the first time in their lives.

Patricia finally understood her brother and her mother. And she even began to understand her father. And most importantly she now understood what being a sister is all about, as well as being a daughter. Her heart felt so big that she could hardly hold it in her body. The lies and deceit between them all. It was because of love and an idea to protect one another as well as their own egos in a twisted world of rules and constructed ideals of value. She accepted the fact that the time had come to leave this cavernous, under ground world to return to the surface, to her Father's world, The Island. She wanted to put a stop to all the maniacal rules that were driving everyone insane. To end both worlds, even if it killed her.

Chapter Ten

～ ～

Loopy handed it to her. The oxygen mask. He smiled this time without black teeth. Jimmy had attached a new tank to it and they placed it on Patricia's face.

"I'm not going to ask where you got this tank, Jimmy."

"Good, then I'm not going to tell you that it's got the poison in it. Sorry, couldn't find anything better."

They looked at each. They both knew the stakes were high. They could only work with what they had. And they had to trust one another when they had never truly trusted before.

Lily had a box for Patricia. "I gathered this just for you, Patricia," she said.

Patricia opened the box. A banana slug. Of course. "Thank you, Lily, Better than flowers." And she kissed Lily on the cheek.

You'll have a full day with this mask. Don't start using it until you get closer to The Island. We'll track you."

"And how will you track me?"

"I have my ways. I don't reveal all my secrets," Jimmy said.

"I'll just simply believe I've got Jimmy Cricket with me," Patricia said. "Promise me when this is all over, one day, you'll just stick me in front of the ocean and let me stare at it for the rest of my life. I want nothing more."

"Time to go."

"What about Mother. I want to say goodbye."

"I don't think she wants to see you right now," Jimmy said.

"What? I'm headed back to do her work and she wants nothing to do with me? Fuck that shit!"

Patricia turned around and started calling. "Mother, where are you?" She stomped through the cave looking for her until Mother came forward.

"It's hard for me, Patricia. As a Mother to know that I brought you into all of this. Please understand."

"I understand. I got it. Don't worry."

And Patricia did get it.

Jimmy led Patricia through the cave, climbing over rocks for what felt like hours, taking breaks to nurture the scrapes they got along the way. There were so many jagged edges and places to slip. But they didn't. And finally after hours of climbing they came to a trap door.

"Tell me I don't have to climb into a redwood tree, Brother."

"No, you're climbing into Father's Tower."

Patricia looked at her brother with jaws wide open. "We are under Father's Tower?"

"Go."

"Patricia put on her mask and prepared to breathe the poison that was part of her Father's world. A control that had been placed on the people for years and they couldn't even see it themselves as they had been breathing it for so long. The lies of protecting the people. And she had to step into the lie to bring truth and free those who were most vulnerable or face her own death. She knew this. And she fully accepted it.

"I've got your back," Jimmy said.

Patricia climbed the stairs and carefully lifted the trap door that led to one of the long corridors of her Father's Nature Center. She started to walk freely amongst the workers there. Nobody even noticed her or could possibly know what she had endured for the last few days. A completely underground secret world. Who could she tell? No one. Not yet.

She noticed, though, how different everyone looked to her. Like robots walking up and down the corridors. Stern looks. Self important. Labels on their clothing to identify status. The absence of thought or question. The network of tubes and pipes that lined the corridor was a bit mirror of the kind of machine the people had become. Their minds dominated by ideas driven into them like a screwdriver works a screw. Their eyes vacant of laughter or even weirdness. Oxygen masks securely fastened, keeping their own viruses to themselves, Patricia thought. It all looked so sterile. Father hadn't saved the world. He had created machines. A woman then looked at Patricia, and she felt uncomfortable. And then someone tapped her from behind.

"Have you been working with the monkeys or the orangutans?" A guard approached her. And she tightened up.

"I know their space had gotten a little dirty, but you need a bath. And you are too dirty to be with everyone. You might spread a disease. Please find the facilities for hygiene right away. There is another class this week on Saturday to ensure you follow the right protocols for hygiene. I suggest you follow up with that."

She knew the guard but he didn't recognize her. And she decided to keep it that way. She also knew his words didn't express a suggestion and she could be cited.

"Thank you. I'm headed there now. And I'll be sure to sign up for the class. Thank you." And she walked faster, straight to her Father's Tower where she hoped her room would still be. Where she could decontaminate herself and breathe deep before finding her Father.

How do you describe such a feeling. Washing away filth from the inside out. That's how it felt to Patricia under the shower head. Steam. Breath. It was as if she had never left. Her room was as it was left. Had it bee a dream? As she dried herself in the mirror she looked closely at her face. She seemed so relaxed. So calm. She looked closer. A mole had developed on the side of her cheek. She looked even closer.

"Jimmy?" She smiled. "From crickets to moles. Hi Jimmy." She knew. He was with her. "I swear, when this is all done, micro technology, all of the technology, is going to get stepped on and squished. Did you hear that loud enough? Just like a nasty insect!"

She was ready to present herself to her father.

She walked the long corridors to her father's office. She heard murmuring inside. There he was in a conference with the others. Father looked up to her.

"My dear Patricia. Have a seat. Have you rested well?" he said.

She knew this side of him. The calm, collected side but inside she knew him too.

"Excuse me, Gentleman. I believe we have concluded our meeting. Tonight we will broadcast to The Island our intentions for the next move toward freedom and liberty. Our beloved Island will once again be healthy and be set on a path of integrity."

And they left. Patricia looked at Father and waited. Would he scream? Would he slap her? She was ready for him.

"Tonight I would like you to join me for our weekly broadcast to the beautiful people of our Island, Patricia. I am afraid I've been a bad father."

She watched him. Could it be possible he felt remorse?

"Come. Come. Come see this with me." He flipped a switch to view the cameras on the streets. The cameras in the homes. The cameras on the drones. The cameras everywhere. "Beautiful people, don't you think? Do you see them walking safely with their children? Do you see them at peace?"

She didn't answer. Where was he going with this?

He flipped another switch and it showed the people in the Recovery Center. Together in a large room were a collection of old people in wheelchairs. Some missing legs. Others screaming to walls. Filthy younger people who were ripping clothes off themselves. One hit a legless old man.

"Angry people who don't respect. They don't respect themselves. They don't respect life. They don't respect anything. We've tried everything. Education. Discipline. Medication. In the end, I am the one who helped save the people who actually care." Then he looked at Patricia. "Why don't you push that button, Patricia?"

She looked at the red button and that feeling came to her. That gut feeling her mother always talked about. Stick with your gut.

"No thank you. And why are they all in the same room? I've never seen that before."

Father looked at Patricia hard. He turned off the screen. "Perhaps you are right. One can always learn. And maybe you needed to teach me a lesson. You always were a good girl, weren't you?"

"Why did you rape me?" Patricia stood stern. Now, it was her turn to look bold on the outside while her insides twisted and turned. She looked at him hard.

Father looked away. "Do you know what madness is like? Do you know what it's like to lose your mind and give that power to someone you think you can trust? To someone you love?" He looked at her. I casted her away. Far away. She was the one who lured me and I promised after that to never ever allow anyone to have power over you, Patricia. I have built this entire world for you. All for you. Do you have any idea how much I have sacrificed for you? And I trusted you. I didn't give you the same chip that others are required to have deep in their bodies, to help keep them safe. The oxygen we produced when they were sharing diseases, killing each other mindlessly? Or the level of technical superiority we gained with implanting chips into the brains of humans to create a world that is more just. Do you have any idea of what The Great Collapse was like? People dying. Millions of animals being slaughtered. Our oceans a disaster. Our very oceans that create the very oxygen we breathe was disrespected, exploited and became diseased because people were insane with greed. People were dying because the air was disappearing."

He slapped his fast on the table. "We saved the world. I saved the world. For you. And I trusted you and you abused my trust."

Patricia rubbed her wrist. Her heart was beating fast. Should she talk about Mother now? Does he know? What does he really know?

The world was a miserable place before we created The Island, FAN Inc and MOO. And all of this is yours, Patricia. All of it."

"I don't want it." She had the courage to say it. "I don't want anymore lies. I don't want to kill anyone. You just tried to make me kill those people with that red button. How dare you." She held firm. Was this the moment to be prepared for? She thought of what Jimmy must be thinking, watching from the mole on her cheek. Could she trust her brother to help her in her time of need?

Father sat down in the chair. It squeaked. "Okay. I've done what I can. I'm not going to do anymore. Perhaps you are right."

He looked defeated. Was he actually being honest? Was he changing?

"How about this. Tonight you join me on our broadcast. The people of our Island World would love to see you anyway." He chuckled. "You're a much prettier face than this old man with a diseased heart, chips for brains and iron hips. Come tonight, Patricia. It's time we move on. Go rest and be ready. I want you to know that I listen to you." And he left.

That evening Patricia put on her lipstick. She walked into Great Room. There was Father. Alone in front of the screen. He stood and walked toward her. "I do love you dear. We'll make this special."

What did he mean? She was ready for anything.

He seemed so poised. Well dressed and put together. Calm. "It's time."

They sat together at a table while the cameras were set and the programming streamed with a voice "Five seconds."

Patricia licked her lips. What was Father going to say?

"Dear great people of The Island. I welcome you to another broadcast by MOO and FAN, Inc., the agencies that bring to you your comfort and joy. For nearly thirty years we have tried our best to ensure you safety, your fresh air and your disease free world. We have done our best. And I'm so happy to announce tonight that we have reached a carbon level unlike any recorded in sixty years. We are past climate change. You have all sacrificed well. Your children will remember you as the saviors of our great planet which is filled with our beautiful animals roaming free as they were meant to be. I personally thank you.

Tonight also marks another special occasion. My dear daughter Patricia is here with me and speaks with concern about those who need our help. The Indigents, those who have always needed our help on a greater level. And we have done our best to help them. Always. So, tonight, my friends, we have just released them to all to the streets so their economic drain on the economy will be no more. But, that is not all, my dear Island friends, my dear daughter Patricia wants to stand united "with the Island people." She has voluntarily chosen to have one of her legs amputated in order to show solidarity with The Indigents. I am so proud of my daughter to show such a resilient measure in order to show her heart and her will. That is all tonight. Have a good night."

Patricia looked at her Father. "What the hell?"

A team of people came in within moments and took Patricia. She started to scream. "I hate you, Father. How dare you!"

Her father switched the screen to the street cameras. Violence was erupting on the streets. And he shed a tear.

"I thought this is what you wanted?"

And then he looked at the officials. "Be prepared to leave in one hour. We go to The Wildlands tonight. It's time."

"You knew?"

"I know everything."

Patricia screamed. "You can't get away with this!"

Father looked out the window. Another tear dropped from his eye. "You have no idea how much I sacrificed for you, Patricia."

"Cyrus. Please cut off the air to the people."

The violence in streets erupted. But then something else happened too.

Lily appeared in the streets. She had a box. "Banana Slugs! They're free! Take a banana slug!"

Jimmy was there too. Along with Loopy and all the others. Running through the streets. And like many of those released from the Recovery Center, they grabbed the boxes and started to pass the banana slugs to the people.

"Lick the banana slugs! It's freedom!"

Father looked at the screen. "What the hell?"

Patricia removed her mask. And opened the box she was carrying. "I'm free too!." And she licked the banana slug in front of her father.

"What the fuck?" He looked at the other members of MOO. Patricia ripped the mask off the man who was holding her and he started to cough.

"You lied! You poisoned our air!" She ran out of the room.

Father grabbed his heart. "To The Wildlands. Now."

The chaos was enormous. Word was understood quickly in the streets that the banana slugs were the antidote. And for the first time in thirty years people started to dance in the streets. Holding the banana slugs up in the air, a testament to the dawn of new time. But it wasn't complete yet.

The Father drove his large tractor. The one that could lift trees straight out of the earth, one by one, like toothpicks. He raced across The Wildland ready to unearth The Mother.

Patricia and Jimmy chased him through the forest and the crowd from The Island followed like a mob. And then they all came to a stop. The destruction around them. Father ripping trees from the ground one by one.

Jimmy screamed. "Father. Stop! You're going to kill Mother!"

She was in the ground. The trees were being uprooted around her. The roaring of the engine drowned out the screaming of Patricia. "Stop!"

And then Father did stop. Everyone stopped. There was Mother.

She was crawling out of a hole. Covered in dirt. Blood dripping down her face. Birthing from the earth. Her clothing ripped and torn. She crawled slowly. Jimmy moved to run toward her but Patricia stopped him. "Wait. Look at Father."

Father got out of the tractor and moved toward the Mother. Patricia and Jimmy watched.

"Oh my God,"

Mother stands up, squinting her eyes. She rubs her eyes. And, straightens her skirt and her hair. Everyone watches.

"My it's bright out here." She looks around. Why is every one looking at me?

"Harold, did you really have to get so violent? Look what you did to the forest after we worked so hard keeping it so nice.".

Father fell onto the ground and Mother approached him. "Look at the mess you've made. I'm always cleaning up after your, Harold. Always cleaning up. And, you wonder why I left years ago. I had a world to work on. I guess like you too".

The Mother kneeled down toward Father. "Take my heart Betty. Take it. I am so sorry. I am so sorry."

Was it a moment of reconciliation? Or one of fatigue? Was it an awakening? Or it a testament to that moment before death that you recognize love? A look was exchanged between.

Betty leaned closer to Roger. "Couldn't hear you? Speak a little louder."

"Your breath really stinks." he said.

"Well, you aged pretty ugly yourself. What the hell do you want me to do give this disaster you created."

"Wasn't my fault."

There was a smile between the both of them. A pause. A rekindling. And as Patricia listened to their silence, she could understand what they were thinking and wanted.

"They're in love again, do hear them?" Lily pulled on Patricia's shirt.

"What are you saying, Lily?"

"Can't you hear them talking? They are remembering their times together, like when they sat on a grassy hill one sunny day and made you."

Patricia whipped her head toward Lily.

"Tell me more, Lily." And she picked Lily up into her arms and held her tight, maybe like Mother and Father had once done with her when she was a small child. Maybe it was a hug that Patricia needed. Patricia even kissed the head of the doll that Lily held tightly in her hand with the wobbly tooth stuck in its mouth."

"Now they're remembering their wedding and all the friends in their lives before The Great Collapse. The dinners, the laughter and the joy. And they are both about to cry. Now, your dad is remembering when he first met your mother, and she was so beautiful. Your mom is remembering your father when she first saw him and how it took a little bit of time to fall in love, but she did.

"Keep going, Lily."

Now comes the good part. They are getting ready to die and say goodbye. And soon they will be spirits with us everyday!

"What! No!"

"Patricia, they are spirits in human form and they will return to us in the wind. Do you feel the wind now. Those are all the spirits joining us now. It's a celebration!"

"You are a crazy child. No!" Patricia put the child down and ran toward her parents.

"It's time to die, but I can't with this damn pacemaker contraption. They never did get it right. Damn scientists. Patricia, you need to turn it off. It's time. It's time for me to die".

"No! Me first! It's time for me. I've did my best you know." Mother said.

"Will you please stop fighting about who is going to die first for god's sake. NO MORE FIGHTING."

Jimmy came running over to them. "What's happening? Oh, my god, there is blood everywhere."

"Well, it looks like we got a little family meeting, Harold. You always wanted them. What do you want us to do?"

"Jimmy, my son. I was not a good father. You are a good man. Pleae, you must cut my heart out and bury it with your mother. It's time to die."

Mother began to cough up blood. "It's a good day to die."

"No!" Patricia said.

"Look around you, Patricia. The world is yours. And Jimmy's. As brother and sister. Honor it well. Honor each other well.

Lily climbed the nearby oak tree and watched them all as the people of The Island and Mushroom Colony came together. And she began the song. "We are world, we are the people. We are the ones. . . who make a better day. . .

The following day Patricia was laying in the tall grasses with Lily and Jimmy. The community was rebuilding homes, lighting fires, cooking food and collecting plants creating a new world. The sun was glorious on this particular day, reminding Patricia of her grandmother's soft quilt. And she smiled.

Lily was very quiet. Reflective. She was missing Mother. And Patricia knew that. She didn't have to hear the words from Lily this time. Jimmy, too, was quiet but also feeling so free after living in the underground world for so long.

"Lily, do you remember the Willie Wonka cabinet in the Mushroom Colony?"

"Oh, yes. Most of all the things in there were my finders keepers that I shared with the colony. Mother said I was the best eagle eye ever," Lily said with a hint of sadness.

"You never did learn what a Willie is, did you?"

"Nope. I never did."

"Would you like me to show you?" Patricia said smiling.

"Oh, yes, I would!"

And with that permission, Patricia put her index finger in her mouth and and grabbed Lily, holding her tightly. "This is a Wet Willie!" Patricia stuck her wet slobbery finger into Lily's ear and twisted it. "Ew, that's gross!!"

"That my dear is a Wet Willie. Would you like another one?"

"Oh, it's my turn!" Jimmy said. And off Jimmy chased Lily, as they ran through the fields, remembering and honoring the joy of play and trust. Patricia stood in those fields that day mesmerized by the moving grasses, the dance of nature. And she began to move her body in a new way, remembering to always remember.

And that my friends, was not the end, but the very beginning.

The Beginning.

Afterword

The idea of mental illness in the way I wrote is not to be ill considered. In fact, there are many shamans and healers today who say that the mentally ill, as we call people in the west, who fill our institutions or even prisons, are actually "healers." those who are highly sensitive to the energy around them. And yet, they are the ones who are usually most abused, locked up in prisons and misunderstood.

One particular Shaman Malidoma Patrice Some from the Dagara tribe in Africa, wrote about a visit he made to a mental health clinic. He explained that the natural born healers of our society are not taught their strength and their gifts are ignored. He says there are no mentally ill in his tribe.

The idea of the whispering trees and Earth is also not my imaginary construct in this story. It is merely an idea I have passed along that was shared in the book *Wise Women of the Dreamtime: Aboriginal Tales of the Ancestral Powers*, a Collection by K. Langloh Parker. The Kogi of Columbia say they can hear Mother Earth calling for help. They had tracked down a British Filmmaker twice and made the most recent film *Aluna*, as a warning to the world. Jane Goodall wrote about a story in her book *Seeds of Hope: Wisdom and Wonder from the World of Plants*. She describes a story about a man who falls asleep by a tree and wakes up with a song in his mind. He plays that song for the local native American tribe and an elder of that tribe says to him that they were well in tune with the tree of that particular song.

The scientist and writer Monica Gagliano wrote a book called *Thus the Plant Spoke* citing her research the bioacoustics of plants and ground breaking work, on a shamanic level, of plant communication and intelligence.

In the 1977 the published work *Kundalini - Psychosis of Transcendence* by Lee Sannella, M.D., has been highly revered. Sannella reveals the forgotten or ignored concept of Kundalini that which dates back to the Ancient Vedas. Sannella writes that we in the modern society have been so desensitized to our feelings that they've been virtually knocked out of us at a very early age.

"In our studies, we have observed the development of these intuitive powers as a difficult and painful rebirth occurring later in life, and even then only in rare individuals. But in certain primitive tribes such as the bushmen and aborigines these abilities develop easily and naturally from childhood onwards. Why should people in the West need two births to claim this natural birthright? This suggests that the intuitive mechanism must be reborn because it has in the meantime "died"– or, to put more bluntly, it has been killed."

The idea about society being drugged up with mental health pharmaceuticals is not that far from our current standard in the United States. As a teacher I constantly hear children who I would deem as simple, normal, energetic children being advised to take drugs "so they can manage themselves," a direct quote from an eleven year old girl I once meant. It's become a crisis, as shown in a powerful documentary called *Generation RX* by Kevin P. Miller. It would not be a radical statement to say that the "state of childhood has become a disease" that needs to be medicated to ensure parents and schools can maintain a semblance of success? One would never want to blame a high level school or wealthy parents for not ensuring a child's success, or whatever that word has now come to symbolize.

I think of my own childhood. I was highly, almost dysfunctionally, shy. I was dirty and proud of my black foot status as the end of summertime camping each year. Later I became highly challenging, angry and am surprised I survived my teen years through self sabotaging means, whether through drugs or pushing safety issues. My parents were always nonjudgmental and stood by me, constantly, with love. My reasons for behavior? I was a highly sensitive child and I saw so many of the injustices around me, whether televised famine images from Africa or being forced to do work at school which I hated. I couldn't understand my anger until I was older and looked back at a societal culture that would worship boys in tights violently competing in a field to get a ball in a goal but would judge it wrong to dance with friends on a Friday night at a club, with poetic, soulful music highlighting songs of humanity. In the 1980s, indeed, the world was mad, and Tears for Fears, New Order and others helped me make sense of it all and later connected me to high literature in college. In my early twenties, still beholden to pushing safety issues, I traveled solo to Central America, sat on top of a Mayan Temple in Guatemala and asked myself how it was possible that I never once learned in my entire education about the constructs of these Mayan Indigenous Cultures just south of my border. I felt robbed of an education and had simply endured an engine of fast foods, corporate money agendas and institutional power. And our society has grown far worse today.

I came across all these books and films by happenstance. Some were merely left in a box as giveaways on a sidewalk or perhaps I was invited to friend's house to see the powerful about the Kogi and their message in the film Aluna. Through these collective experiences and works I began to observe a growing narrative that helped explain a powerful episode in my own life journey and solidified an explanation from a spiritual friend who remarked to me "nothing is coincidental".

Just a few years prior I had experienced what some might call "Kundalini" which procured a powerful feeling of attachment to forces of energy around me, including what was like a whispering all around me, that I would not otherwise hear, including even words from my passed uncle. I actually thought I was going insane.

It followed a divorce that was extraordinarily painful. "Trauma" is one of the many paths yogis have said can lead to Kundalini, a break with your old path and resetting of a new one tapping into your natural gifts, your sensitivity, a spiritual awakening, as described in the book *Kundalini: Psychosis or Transcendence?* I was able to isolate myself for several weeks during this state. It was most frightening because I felt I was suspended in between two worlds, ours and an etherial one that felt absolutely infinite, a magnetic force of colors and timelessness. I did not want to leave this state and I felt connected to it because of my Great Uncle who I felt holding me the entire time, with pure love, as if there was a message I needed to share and a journey I needed to take. There were no psychedelics or alcohol or coffee. And for the most part, I hardly ate or drank anything. My own energy felt like it extended beyond my body. There was a feeling of utter freedom and pure love except I knew I needed to leave that other world to return to normal life. I had to say goodbye to my uncle and I could feel him telling me that I had a hard journey ahead of me, but he would be with me. I said goodbye to him and I finally felt released.

Following that time, a creative force was also released in me, leading to cathartic writing of three books, a Masters Degree in Humanities, the making of two international films (first time ever), a television program about the environment, and political events leading to the recognition of President Jimmy Carter and more international events that I would have never believed possible. I had also started this novel which was literally flowing out of me at the time, all within five years. A journey began that I could never ever plan.

My great uncle had been a tremendous guide for me. While alive, I had spent time just hanging in his living room eating tuna fish sandwiches and talking politics. We argued intensely, as our views were contrary to one another. But we always got closer because of it, respecting one another. After my uncle's death, I retreated without attending his funeral, opting for a hike in the quiet woods. I swear he was with me. I could "feel" him. And I honored that feeling. I kept him in mind always, along with the many stories he had shared with me and interests he had in his own life. His wife, whom he had adored, had died years before. Her ashes had been scattered on the mountain of my community, a mountain named Mount Tamalpais, a Miwok word meaning "Sleeping Maiden." And I could see the mountain from my window. I thought of her often. And I also thought about how much he had loved her.

My uncle had offered me sailing lessons, a passion he had in life, but I had turned down the gift. After his death I took up lessons which turned into my own passion. The connection to the San Francisco Bay and the Pacific Ocean became my teachers, a meditative practice of finding the balance with the elements of wind and water, always seeking that "groove" as we call it in sailing, where your sails and your boat are in perfect harmony with the forces. Sailing provides a powerful connection with nature and it ultimately gave me a resounding encouragement to trust my abilities, love for the water and freedom that comes with confidence and self determination.

From such feelings as experiencing what could be called a blast of light in my body to hearing voices around me to sitting on a shoreline and feeling wind go right through my body, I couldn't talk about it to anyone with thinking I would sound insane. But yet they were so powerful, I began to grow convinced that I needed to believe in my feelings and follow them no matter what. I had to follow my "gut" going forward.

It wasn't but days after this that I walked along the road to see a martial arts class under our local Redwoods. It was a voice in my body that told me to approach the class when logic would advice me not to. On the outside, my life was a disaster, I was broke, in debt, deep with mediators, lawyers and and a horrific divorce. My children were an emotional wreck. One more thing in my life to ponder was not what any sane person would advise. But I ignored that logic and I watched the class.

The teacher had studied in China by an acclaimed master. The art was all about energy and using that balance of energy to protect yourself. He invited me into the martial arts circle and described our three forces of energy to consider. One is of the mind, which is not always true. The second is our heart which is strong. The third of the gut which is the direct link to the infinite, god or the universe, however you'd like to describe that force with words.

The gut. And I was more convinced thereafter to only use my gut feelings which I pursued with the film projects, writing projects and other intentions that I have had my whole life, including teaching and gardening. Each time I was at the end, believing that I might have made a mistake with my thinking, I would be reminded in subtle ways that I would be okay and I was.

We are at a crossroads today, a time to heal our collective spirits and to ease the burden of guilt, fear and anger. When I found my own moment of release of these feelings, the colors, the sounds and the magic of the universe opened up to me in a feeling of pure love and nonjudgment. I was sitting on a boat, alone in a slip, during the dawn hours of San Francisco. I woke early after many dreams to see what looked like a fiery light shining through the portholes. I emerged from the boat to see the most illuminating sunrise splashing against the water surrounding me. But it wasn't just the colors. The energy was so strong that

I could feel a love unlike any other. And the embrace of this moment and the release of all my old negative feelings revealed to me the world beyond all that was ever told to me. And to believe.

Life is sacred and magic is alive.

And please know, not a single banana slug was harmed in the making of this story nor is this story encouraging any banana slug harm. It's just a story. Honor banana slugs.